WHISTLE
PASS
KevaD

Dreamspinner Press

Published by
Dreamspinner Press
382 NE 191st Street #88329
Miami, FL 33179-3899, USA
http://www.dreamspinnerpress.com/

Whistle Pass

Cover Art by Anne Cain   annecain.art@gmail.com
Cover Design by Mara McKennen

ISBN: 978-1-61372-376-0

Printed in the United States of America
First Edition
February 2012

eBook edition available
eBook ISBN: 978-1-61372-377-7

To Robert and my other friends who asked this story be written.

CHAPTER 1

September 1955

CHARLIE HARRIS leaned forward, pinched the end of the Lucky Strike between his thumb and forefinger, and inhaled the last drag possible before the smoldering tobacco burned his lips. Easing the smoke out his nostrils, he dropped the stub to the floor and ground it out with the sole of his boot. The carcass joined the other dozen or more shredded on the floor of the bus.

He sat back, rubbed the two-day stubble, coarse as sandpaper, on his cheek, and inhaled the garbage stench of smoke, sweat, banana peels, and God knew what else the other passengers had stuffed in the paper sacks they'd leave for somebody else to clean up. The kid wearing the coonskin cap and Davy Crockett fringe coat, curled up asleep in the seat across the aisle, had peanut butter and jelly smeared around his mouth like cheap lipstick. Why the mother didn't clean the crap off the brat was beyond him. Maybe she'd tired of his incessant running up and down the walkway, too, and was afraid to touch him for fear of an encore.

Charlie turned his head and stared at the window. The low light from the recessed lamp above him, under the luggage rack, illuminated his dark hair. His haloed reflection stared back against the pitch of the moonless night. Drops of drizzle running down the glass in rivulets disfigured his features, but not the memories. He shifted in his seat, resting his cheek on the backrest.

Need you had been the only words on the telegram—not an *I want you* stuck anywhere on the yellow paper. The first time Roger had said, "Need you," Charlie'd fallen into his arms and bared his heart, soul, groin, and ass.

He dug the open pack of Luckies out of a pocket in his pea coat, shook the end of one out, and held it between his teeth. He returned the dwindling cache to the pocket, pulled out a book of matches, folded the cover behind a lone match with one hand, and scratched it across the striker without tearing it from the pack. The tobacco sizzled as he inhaled. He blew out the match flame when he exhaled and watched the smoke bounce off his reflection.

What was it? Nine years? No. Ten. Ten years already since the war ended and all the troops came marching home. Those that weren't buried in some rathole of a town he couldn't pronounce the name of in some European country he never wanted to see again. He blew out another cloud of smoke. He wasn't a twenty-year-old kid anymore. But sure as hell, the minute Roger said, "Need you," he'd walked off his job and caught a bus. For what? A chance of love with a man who'd walked away without looking back when they stormed the beaches of the good old US of A?

"Moron." He rolled his body away from the reflection and stared at the beige metal above him. Another drag, another burst of smoke.

Lightning shattered the darkness. Thunder clapped against the bus. Raindrops transformed to a hail of rifle and machine gun bullets.

Charlie jerked. His eyes prowled the terrain for where the Germans' attack would come from—*goddamnit! It's just rain.* He fell back against the seat, brushed a jittery hand over his hair, and took a long, comforting pull off the cigarette. So long ago, so damn long ago, and still it took so little to bring the horror back to life.

"Whistle Pass. Whistle Pass," the driver called out.

Charlie sat straight, grateful for something else to fill his mind with, and looked over the top of the wide brim hat of the passenger in the seat in front of him. Through the windshield eight rows away, a smattering of lights appeared in the distance. He crinkled his nose. Figured. He'd guessed a town in Illinois called Whistle Pass a hundred-fifty miles or so from Chicago wouldn't be more than a pinhole on a map. By the few lights, he'd nailed it.

He narrowed his focus and strained in an attempt to look beyond the glare of the glass and drizzling rain but couldn't make out anything except the glow of random streetlights as the bus entered the city. A porch light here and there indicated houses along the street. The bus rounded a slow curve, and a lone parking lot light's glow illuminated jewels of rain on wet cars. A string of multicolored triangular banners hung limp. A dealership. He sat back and took in the blur of more houses.

The bus rounded another lazy curve, and the downtown spread her Main Street curbing like a whore. Each block had streetlamps strategically interspersed so every storefront was revealed. Vaughan's Saddle and Tack, Goldman Jewelers, A&P Grocery, Ash Penn's Stationery, Matson Jewelers…. Charlie chuckled. The business district looked about five blocks long, and two jewelry stores were battling it out for control of the bangle industry.

A hiss from the brakes. The bus slowed and pulled to the curb in front of a four-story building. A giant L with "Hotel" painted down the stem of the letter hung from an iron bracket. Rain dripped to the sidewalk from the base of the sign.

Charlie pushed out of his seat. In the aisle he rolled cramped shoulders, flexed the stiffness out of a knee, and combed his fingers through his hair before he retrieved his duffle from the overhead. The fact he was the only passenger to do so didn't escape his notice. He pinched out the final draw of nicotine from the cigarette between his lips. Dropping the remnant to the floor, he opted to step over, not on, the butt and strode to the front of the bus.

The driver pushed the handle of the extended bar of the door, and Charlie stepped out onto the wet sidewalk. Drizzle quickly painted his face. A drop fell from the tip of his nose. He swiped the next one and took a deep breath. The air was clean, but beneath the overlay of rain was a taste of fish. Dead fish. He inhaled another lungful of air. Yeah. A river was somewhere close by.

Gears hissed into place. The engine revved, and the bus drove off. Diesel fumes encased in a swell of black smoke threatened to cloak Charlie. He stepped toward the building, away from the bus's lingering stink. The wood-framed glass door had "Larson Hotel" painted in gold with black trim. He pulled it open, hoping they'd have a room available. If they didn't, he was pretty much screwed.

He guessed the lobby's ceiling to be around twelve feet with three ceiling fans suspended on pipes to about eight feet. Four black couches, a few wooden armchairs, and potted plants here and there decorated the place. At the far end of the room, the elevator's iron gate stood open, the operator's stool empty. A solitary broad-chested man puffing on a cigar sat on a couch. A snap-brim hat pulled low shadowed his face. Smoke curled upward, only to be blown back down by the fan blade's slow rotation. To the right of the elevator was a wooden stairway, the banister nearly black from decades of hands sliding over it. A grandfather clock in a corner tolled 3:00 a.m.

Charlie turned left to the long, dark wood counter. A bank of pigeonholes, several with keys, was mounted to the wall. He smiled. Keys in the slots meant there was probably a vacancy. With the office chair at the desk unoccupied, he slapped a palm onto the silver bell. The clang rolled around the room. A pair of curtains parted, and an old man walked out.

"Morning. Sorry. No trains due in, so I was laying down." He looked around and lowered his voice. "Most of our guests work for the railroad. Railroad changes crews in Whistle Pass. Not many tourists of late. Looking for a room? Don't have much right now, though."

Charlie set his bag on the floor. "Yeah. Whatever you have's fine."

The old man set a book on the counter. Opening it, he handed Charlie a pen. "Need you to register. How long you staying?"

Charlie wrote his name underneath a bevy of names without addresses. "Not sure. You need my address?"

The old man plucked a key from a slot and pivoted back around. "Not really. Nobody's business but yours. That's the way I see it, anyway. Manager tends to disagree, though, unless you work for the railroad, of course." He flashed a wry smile. "But he ain't here, is he?" He spun the book around and started to close it but paused. "Charlie Harris?"

Charlie tensed. The whiskey-dry voice spoke his name like the employee recognized it. "Yeah. Why?"

The clerk turned, set the key back in the slot, and pulled another one from a different hole. He handed the key to Charlie. "Had a note to expect you sometime tonight. Room 412's reserved for you. Paid in advance for a week."

Confused, Charlie looked at the brass tag with a machine-pressed L and 412. "Who got me a room?" *And why a week?* Not like the Roger he knew to have things planned out in advance.

"Don't know. Note didn't say. You can ask the manager when he comes in later. Need help with your bags?"

Charlie picked up the duffle. "Nah. I got it."

"Good, 'cause I couldn't help you anyway. You'll have to use the stairs. I'm not allowed to leave the lobby since I'm the only one working. So there's nobody to run the elevator."

An amused snort leaked out of Charlie. The old man couldn't leave the lobby unattended, but he could steal a few winks in the back room. He wheeled and noticed the sitting area was now empty.

The thick leather soles of his work boots clunked echoes as he walked up the stairs. Curtains of fresh cigar smoke hung in the air. On the second floor, Charlie made the turn and spotted half a cigar smoldering in a pedestal ashtray. The band identified it as a Red Dot. He glanced up and down the hallway but didn't see anything that seemed out of place, other than a wasted choice smoke. He cocked his head and listened. Nothing. Unbuttoning his coat, he headed for the third floor landing.

On the third floor, he stalled his progress and looked and listened again. A stuttered snoring crawled along the empty hall. Charlie shook his head and blew out a breath. "You're just nervous about why you're here. Shake it off." He grabbed the banister and pulled himself up the stairs, his booted steps rhythmically clomping his advance. At the midway point, he palmed the ball on the banister break and made the turn.

A Black Cat shoe heel came at him too quickly for Charlie to react. The blow caught him between the eyebrows.

Charlie slammed against the wall. Pain exploded in his head. Blinded from shock, he swung the duffle. The weight of the bag in his left hand pulled him to his right, so he let go of it, balled a fist, and blasted it back across his front. The backhand blow struck pay dirt in a jaw. The attacker cursed. Charlie followed up with a right fist to the shadowy figure coming into focus. His fist hammered into a rib cage. Charlie pumped two more quick jabs into the ribs.

"Gack." The man's torso leaned left.

Charlie reached out, grabbed two handfuls of shirt, and flung the man past him, into the wall. Staying with his target, he planted his feet and loosed a flurry of punches onto the exposed back, over the kidneys.

The snap-brim-hatted attacker's knees bent, and he sank to the floor.

Click. Click. Charlie whirled. At the top of the stairs, two more men. Young. Late teens, early twenties maybe. Each wore blue jeans and a black leather jacket, and... each held a switchblade knife.

"Enough of this crap." Charlie snarled, stuck his left hand into his coat pocket, and pressed the barrel of the gun against the cloth. "First lesson, assholes. Never bring a knife to a gunfight."

The two youths froze in place. They exchanged looks. One turned and ran. The other, red hair swept back under layers of grease, gulped a prominent Adam's apple, then took off in the direction of the first.

Charlie bolted up the stairs, rounded the turn to the hallway, and saw the young men scamper out an open door at the end of the hall. He scrambled to the open exit and found himself at the top of an iron fire escape. The clanking footfalls of the duo were already two floors below him.

Charlie stood and waited. The two men hit the alley and continued running. He pulled the hand gun from his pocket, took careful aim, and fired.

"Bang. Bang," he softly said, then he blew on the fingernail of his index finger gun barrel. "Idiots."

He went inside the hotel to the stairway. The first one, the cigar smoker, was gone as well. He retrieved his duffle, located room 412 next to the fire escape, and unlocked the door.

Charlie set the duffle on the metal-framed bed and went back to the hall. The bathroom was across from his room. His brows rose in satisfaction. Entering the water closet, he pulled the dangling chain. A bare, single lightbulb clicked on in a ceiling lamp. In the small mirror on the wall, he examined his face. Not bad. The blow had struck more forehead than anything else. He rubbed the reddened skin, then turned on the faucet, cupped his hands full of cool water, and lightly scrubbed his face. He grabbed the sides of the sink and stared at his reflection. His jaw trembled, his teeth chattered, his gut knotted, and his chest tightened. He flung his arms around him and sat on the toilet, shaking in fear.

In the war, he'd reacted the same way. Always calm when the shit went down, and always fell apart after. The men around him had learned to stick to him when the bullets flew. Charlie Harris could fight and shoot. You wanted to live, you needed to be wherever Charlie was. Only Roger ever sat with him after. Only Roger ever put his arms around him and held him until the terror passed.

He closed his eyes. How he wanted Roger's arms around him right now, his breath on his skin, the taste of him on his lips. A tear rolled down his cheek.

The door swung open. "You Harris?"

Charlie looked up. A uniformed cop stood in the doorway, badged cap resting at an angle on the man's head. Still shaking, Charlie only nodded.

The cop walked to him, placed a hand under his arm, and helped him to stand. "Come on. Let's get you to your room."

Grateful, Charlie staggered to his room. The door clicked closed behind him. Charlie sat on the bed, his hands stuck between his thighs as he tried to control the tremors. The cop walked over and stood in front of him. Charlie glanced up. "Did someone call you? I got attacked on the stairs."

The cop reached into a pocket sewn into the lower leg of the dark blue uniform trousers and produced a leather sap. "Nobody called me, boy." The cop reared back and slapped the lead-filled sap across Charlie's thigh.

Charlie screamed in pain.

"Shut up," the cop growled, and he hit his thigh again.

Pain seared, burned through his bones. Charlie fell back on the bed. Tears flowed, snot rolled out of his nose. He wanted to puke. He stuffed a hand in his mouth and bit into it to muffle his cries.

The cop hit his thigh again. Then again.

Charlie went fetal, whimpering. He clamped his eyes closed against the twisting daggers flowing through his blood, shredding his nerves, clawing at his brain.

A whisper at his ear. "You watch yourself, boy. One step—just one step—out of line, and you'll be turtle food."

The sap bludgeoned his thigh again. Charlie dug his teeth into his hand. Blood washed over his gums and tongue. The door opened and closed.

Charlie pulled his knees even tighter to his chest and sobbed. "Roger. Where are you?"

CHAPTER 2

IN THE covered doorway of the hotel's entrance, Gabe Kasper shook the rain off his fedora. Looking toward the river a mere block and a half beyond the street corner the hotel rested on, he frowned. The rain veiled the city park housing a gravel lot for boat trailers. The barely visible edge of the river at the docks was flannel gray.

"Damn."

For once, the weathermen had been right, and on the wrong weekend—opening day of goose season. Not even geese hunters would come out in this soup. You can't shoot what isn't there to kill. The geese would all be hunkered down in fields and around marshy ponds until the skies cleared and they could continue their southbound exodus.

A shrill, air-powered whistle scratched through the air. Gabe waited. A second, though an octave lower, whistle soon followed. Two freighters employing a tradition started by the now long-gone paddlewheel riverboats. The deep-water channel narrowed in the middle of the river. On days like this, where the captains couldn't see each other, they whistled their presence. The freighters would hug the channel's starboard edges to avoid colliding.

The sternwheeler captains had dubbed it a "whistle pass."

Gabe sighed at the prospect of low revenues and opened the door. "Morning, Mrs. Brewer."

The silver-haired woman looked up from the lobby counter. "Good morning, Mr. Kasper. Eight cancellations so far."

As expected. He strode around the end of the counter. "When are you going to call me Gabe while we're at work?"

She continued dusting and tidying up the work area. "When you start calling me Olga."

He slipped off his coat and hung it on a peg, then set his hat to dry on top of the oak filing cabinet. He gently touched palms to the sides of his hair, ensuring no strands were out of place. "But your name isn't Olga, it's Betty."

She snapped the cloth. Dust billowed in the air. Gabe watched it float back onto the area the pillow-shaped woman had just cleaned.

"Why do you do that? Why do you refuse to shake the rag outside like I've asked you to?"

She brushed past him. "Job security."

He chuckled. "I could fire you for not following instructions, you know."

She stopped, turned, and patted his cheek. "You couldn't replace me. Nobody else would put up with your attitude."

His brow dropped. "Attitude? I don't have an attitude."

Bzz, Bzzz. The elevator's buzzer meant a guest was ready to come downstairs.

"I have to go to work. Maybe you should think about actually earning your pay, Mr. Kasper." Betty waddled off, wiping chairs and sofa backs as she made her way to the elevator. She closed the iron gate, sat on the stool, and pulled the metal handle of the controls.

Gabe watched the elevator rise and disappear. Every manager of the Larson soon learned Betty Brewer came with the upholstery. As far back as anyone still living could remember, the Larson had been her one and only job. The restaurant next door ran a pool for the person who could get Betty to reveal her true age. Last time he'd checked, there was $164.35 up for grabs. Two of it had come from his unsuccessful attempt.

He parted the curtains and entered the back room. The down cushions on the couch were dented. Edgar, the night man, had napped again. When the new factory opened its doors, employment had spiked. Recently retired from the railroad, Edgar had been the only applicant for the hotel's night job. The man hadn't missed a shift in three years, and the till was never so much as a nickel off. A few catnaps had become acceptable activity.

Gabe fluffed each cushion to perfection, then nodded approval at the couch. He walked over to the dressing mirror, checked the knot of his red tie, straightened his vest, and inspected the sleeves of his white shirt for any discoloration—his personal morning appraisal. He patted his sculpted black hair, though it clearly didn't need it, the final touch before starting his duties.

Returning to the front desk, he picked up the telephone receiver, tapped the cradle three times, and waited for the operator to come on the line.

"Good morning, Gabe."

"Morning, Ruby. Can you connect me to the Burlington, and then the Milwaukee?" With the hunters' room cancellations, he'd have to offer the vacancies to the railroads at a two-thirds discount to buffer the loss of weekend receipts.

"I already called the yard offices for you, Gabe. What with the rain and fog, I figured you'd be needing the railroad business."

The telephone operator's forethought brought a smile to his lips. "Thank you, Ruby. Stop in sometime and I'll buy you lunch next door."

"I'd prefer buttered popcorn and a helping of Johnny Wayne. Fred over at the theater says he got his hands on a bootleg copy of *Hondo* and is going to show it again for a few days next week."

Gabe chuckled. "Tell you what. I'll talk to Fred and make arrangements for you, Bill, and all three of your children to have reserved seats the first night. I'll even throw in a soft drink. How'd that be?"

Glee percolated out of the phone. "Oh, honey. You just made me one happy mama. You know, Mary Singleton's cousin's coming to town next week. Read it in the paper. Maybe I could get you an introduction. They say she's very charming."

The elevator clanged to a stop. Gabe shifted and looked left. "I have to go, Ruby. A manager's work is never done." He hung up before the woman could expand on the pointless attempt at fixing him up. Ruby wasn't the only one who'd tried since he'd come home. And, regrettably, she probably wouldn't be the last. A single man in such a small town set tongues wagging. Betty slid the scissor gate open.

Gabe's chest froze. He nervously picked at his index nail with his thumb. The man stepping out of the elevator was... gorgeous, in a primitive sort of way.

The man's unshaven jaw was as square as a right angle. Cave-dark eyes under heavy brow foliage. Thin, tight lips. Thick chocolate hair in need of pruning, a curled strand defiantly hung loose in the middle of the stony forehead. The only flaw to the breathing Rembrandt was a bump on the bridge of the nose, once broken, that obviously hadn't healed properly. Gabe gauged him a solid six feet of as manly as the human form could achieve. Hands shoved deep into the pockets of a buttoned pea coat, the guest glided across the floor, though he wore heavy leather boots under jeans rolled at the cuffs.

Gabe clipped his stare short and tossed open the guest register. One new name had been added during the night. Charlie Harris. The mystery man had arrived. Gabe sucked in a breath. And what a man Charlie Harris was.

"You the manager?" The voice was gruff—sexy gruff—sexy like an orgasmic growl.

Gabe looked up into eyes as chocolate as the mass of hair. Matched hair and eyes. Gabe swallowed hard. Perfection had that effect on him. "Ye... yes, sir." *Compose. Compose, Gabriel. Men like this aren't interested in men.*

"I'm looking for someone."

Of course you are. And, of course, it's not someone like me.

"Roger Black. Heard of him?"

Gabe tried to suppress the surprise. Why didn't this man know Roger? Everyone in Whistle Pass knew Roger Black. "Yes, sir, I know Mayor Black."

The face didn't flinch, but the eyes slitted to predatory. Gabe's toes wiggled in apprehension.

"Mayor, huh." It wasn't a question. "Which way's city hall?"

"Make a left, and it's two blocks down on the other side of the street."

The man turned and walked out the door into the rain. Gabe sighed. He should have offered Harris his hat. At least he'd have had a reason to talk to him again.

CHAPTER 3

HOW a man as good-looking as the manager had landed in Whistle Pass, Charlie had no clue. Nor did he have the time to worry about why he'd noticed. He turned up the collar of his coat and stepped into the rain. The chill of it did little to cool his anger. Mayors ran the cops. One of Roger's own people had beaten him. Question was, if Roger knew about it, had he sent him, and if so, why? A poster in a window caught his attention.

He stopped and took it all in. The poster was a man's smiling face. A little older now, but Charlie knew every feature of this particular face.

Vote
Roger Black
State Representative
Working to Build a Better Tomorrow

Rain pasted his hair to his forehead, ran down his nose. He stuck out his lip and blew some drops off. Hunching his shoulders, he clenched his hands inside his coat pockets and started walking. Roger had a hell of a lot of explaining to do.

Two blocks down, he jogged across the street to a corner brick building. A big-finned Chevy with a round red light mounted on the roof was parked out front. The sign on the door said "Whistle Pass City Hall & Police Dept."

Charlie stood under the canvas awning and stomped the water off him. He was tired and needed sleep. After the beating, he'd stayed awake pacing the floor of his hotel room, walking the hall, so his leg wouldn't stiffen. But the cold and wet were serving notice to his weary joints—he needed a warm bed and rest. He opened the door and entered.

An odor of cigar smoke woke his dull senses. He inhaled the smell through his mouth, rolled his tongue over it, but couldn't be sure the flavor was the same as last night.

The door to his left was labeled "Police Dept." Didn't want any part of that right now. Charlie walked over to a directory mounted on the wall. The mayor's office was on the second floor. He clomped up the stairs. Closed double doors at the top were marked "City Council Chambers." A door to his left had a small sign: "Mayor's Office." He knocked.

"Come on in. It's open." The pleasant voice was a woman's.

Charlie opened the door and walked in. "Is the mayor around?"

The woman looked up from the typewriter on a metal stand. "I'm afraid not. He's attending a function out of town today."

"Raising campaign funds?"

Her features contorted to an unbecoming scowl. "No, sir. He can't legally do that during business hours."

Charlie smirked. "Right. My name's Charlie Harris. Mayor Black and I served in the war together. He didn't happen to leave a message for me by chance, did he?"

The woman twisted her torso, leafed through a stack of papers. "No… I don't see anything with that name on it. And he didn't mention you this morning before he left. Was he expecting you?"

What the hell is going on? "I'll be in town for a few days. Would you let him know I came by?"

"Charlie Harris?" She scribbled on a pad. "Correct?"

"Yeah. I'm staying at the hotel."

"I'll be sure to let him know. Were you two close? I mean, in the war?"

He sniggered. "Yeah. Real close." He turned to leave but stopped midway, his motion snagged by a picture on the wall. The photograph had been taken by a war correspondent who'd happened upon their unit. Eight soldiers had posed for the snapshot. When the day ended, only two remained alive. He placed a fingertip on the glass. "That's me." He slid the unwanted memory to the man at his shoulder. "That's Roger."

"Oh my God. You're *that* Charlie. Roger—Mayor Black, told me how you saved his life."

Ghostly visions sucked his guts into a whirlpool. Trembling rattled his ribs. He needed to get out of there. "Let him know I stopped by." She said something behind him, but he couldn't make out the words. He scurried down the stairs and out the door. He tilted his head back and allowed the rain to wash away the tears.

Thunder cracked. The overcast sky opened its reservoir and heavy rain soaked him, bathed him. Lightning flashed. He whirled full circle, scanning the area. A clap of sound. An explosion of noise. The sky flashed branches of yellow. Charlie threw off his coat, crouched, his eyes frantically searching for where the attack would come from. More explosions. Mortars. Screams chewed his brain.

"We've got to get out of here!"

"No!" Charlie shouted. "Stay low! It's an ambush. You don't know where they are!"

"Run, men! Run! Find cover!"

"No, Lieutenant. Stay low 'til we know!" Charlie pleaded. "Stay low!"

But they didn't listen. They all broke and ran, following the lieutenant, their platoon leader. Even Roger.

Charlie spun around, gritting his teeth. He breathed in and out over his clenched jaw. Machine guns, rifles. Explosions—hand grenades. "Goddamnit!" The LT had led them right into the Germans.

Charlie ran. He vaulted the dead and dying, firing his rifle as he ran. The LT fell. The sergeant fell. Hooper, Calloway, Burns… Roger. They all fell. Except Charlie.

He smashed through the hedgerow. Stunned, the Germans hesitated. Charlie didn't. He fired into them until his rifle emptied. Then he pulled his bayonet and slashed. Blood splattered his face, soaked his clothes.

He tore the German soldiers apart until the gunfire stopped.

HARRIS ripped through the lobby and up the stairs. Gabe jerked at the sight of the man, drenched to the skin. Where was his coat? The guest had left the hotel wearing one.

"What do you make of that?" Betty asked from halfway across the room.

Gabe continued to stare at the empty staircase. "I don't know. It was almost as if someone was chasing him."

"Or he was doing the chasing." Betty, now at his side, placed a hand on his arm. "Maybe he has demons, Gabriel. Not everyone handles their past as well as you. Could be he needs a friend who understands."

Gabe glanced out the corner of his eye. Betty only called him by his Christian name when she wanted to make a motherly point. "What are you suggesting? Are you saying I should go to a guest's room and involve myself in his business?" It just wasn't done. He was the manager of a hotel, not a priest. He couldn't go to the man's room, no matter how titillating the thought might be.

"I'm saying that if you located and returned his coat to him, you might learn why I have to mop up the puddles he left on my clean floor." She slapped his arm and walked away.

Gabe watched her drag the mop and bucket from the utility closet. Maybe Betty had a point. Harris was a guest, after all. The least he could do would be to return the man's coat to him. His gaze returned to the stairs. The image of the man hurling his frame up the steps unsettled Gabe. He'd seen men with such determination before. Most died. The ones who lived were never the same.

After tugging on his coat, he carefully settled his hat to provide the least amount of damage to his hair as possible and headed for the door.

THE pea coat was a mass of wet wool in the intersection. Gabe picked it up, held it out as far from his body as his strength would tolerate, and made his way to Millie's Dry Cleaners. At the clank of the bell over the door, Millie came out of the laundering area.

Gabe's eyes watered from the heavy odor of the shop's chemicals. "I need this soon as you can. It belongs to a guest."

Millie clutched the dripping mess with both hands and assessed the project. "There's a tire track on the back. Gonna take the full hour."

Gabe sat on a metal chair at the plate glass window. "I'll wait."

CHAPTER 4

GABE lightly knocked on the door. Receiving no response, he tapped the wood again with his knuckles. He pressed an ear to the door. No sound of steps coming to inquire who it might be. A click and creak of hinges. Gabe snapped upright.

A man in overalls, carrying a metal lunch pail and lantern, walked out of a room midway down the hall. A railroader.

Cheeks burning, Gabe held up the coat draped on a wooden hanger. "I'm returning this to a guest." Gabe busied himself studying the polish on his shoes until the man descended the stairs. He crinkled his nose in disapproval. The rain had speckled the polish—the Florsheims needed a shine.

Coast clear, he pressed his ear to the wood and rapped on it. "Mr. Harris? Are you in there? Is everything all right, sir?" Nothing.

The remnants of Gabe's potatoes and eggs breakfast soured in his belly. This was so wrong, so insane, so… out of his realm of comfort. He pulled the master key from his pocket and unlocked the door. Grasping the brass knob, he turned it, gave it a light push. The door opened a crack. He peered into the room.

Harris, still clad in the wet clothes, was laid out crossways on the bed. Gabe pushed the door wide open. The man's shoulders were off the mattress, his arms dangling in the air along with his head. The eyes were open in a blank stare. Gabe sucked in breath. "Oh shit. He's dead."

He ran to Harris and grabbed the man to lift him onto the covers. Fingers clamped onto Gabe's throat, choking off his ability to breathe. Gabe felt his eyes bulge out, his heart drum with terror.

"You've got three seconds to tell me why you're prowling around my room before I kill you."

He tried to respond, but words couldn't rise past the lock on his throat. Little squeaks leaked out his mouth.

Harris rolled around and sat on the edge of the bed. "You're the hotel manager." He turned Gabe loose. "What are you doing in here?"

What Gabe really wanted to do in here was piss all over the floor and relieve the fear pulsing through him. He inhaled deeply, rubbing his throat. "I thought you were dead. I was just trying to help."

"Not outside the door you weren't. I heard you out there. What do you want?"

Realizing his hands were empty, feeling the ultimate fool, Gabe looked to the doorway. His cheeks and ears burned in embarrassment. The coat lay in a heap where he'd dropped it. "I was returning your coat to you. I had it cleaned." He shuffled over and picked up the pea coat, patted off any invisible dirt that might have attached to it. "No charge. The Larson is only too pleased to...." Gabe looked at Harris, and the rest of his words trailed off, unspoken.

Harris had slumped forward, chin on chest, his hands between his legs. The man was pale as unglazed porcelain. His fingers trembled, then shook violently. The tremors climbed his arms to his shoulders, to his chest, and found their way to his thighs and knees.

"Mr. Harris?" Gabe closed the door and hung the coat and hanger on an iron hook screwed into the back of the door. "Mr. Harris?"

The man's entire body convulsed. Eyelids blinked in rapid succession. Teeth chattered.

"What's wrong with you?" But inside, he knew. Shellshock wasn't anything he hadn't seen before. He heaved a breath and walked to the bed. There he threw the wet spread and top sheet to the floor. "Forgive me, Mr. Harris, but we've got to get you out of these wet clothes."

Gabe tugged off the ribbed T-shirt, the only shirt the man was wearing. He paused, open-mouthed, at the spectacle scarring the man's shaking, muscled body. "What hell did you fight your way out of?" He gently lowered Harris to the bed.

His vision traced the four-inch zippered scar between abdomen and ribcage—bayonet? Three small marks dotted the leathery skin—bullet wounds. Harris was a veteran. Had to be. But from which war? The world war, or Korea? Gabe chewed a lip. Did it really matter? Harris needed help, not dissection.

He hurried to a vacant room and yanked off the spread and top sheet. In 412, he lightly tucked the ends under the mattress. He untied and removed Harris's boots. They weighed a ton. Definitely not like any available around Whistle Pass. He grabbed the socks and stared, impressed, as he pulled them off. The wool socks were bone dry.

He leaned his head back and looked at the ceiling, unsure if he could or should proceed further. A soot cobweb swayed from the plaster. He frowned. Arlene, the upper floors housemaid, wasn't doing her job as he required it be done. He'd have to talk with her about this. Cobwebs, insect or coal-furnace created, were completely unacceptable in the rooms. Gabe rolled his eyes and moaned.

Though Arlene needed a talking to, she had nothing to do with the current dilemma. He dropped his gaze to the quivering body in front of him, the thin layer of chest hair cascading to the navel, breaking the flow, then reforming to a singular trail of fur that disappeared beneath the water-darkened denim over abdomen muscles so developed he could count each one.

Compose, Gabriel. Compose. He's just a man. Albeit one of the most exotic and enticing men you've ever seen, but, still, just a man. Get over it!

Squinting, as if that would minimize the scene, he gingerly unbuttoned the metal button and unzipped the jeans. He grabbed handfuls of the cuffs and pulled. The jeans slid off, and Gabe's jaw dropped. "What the hell?"

The man's left thigh under the boxers was nearly black. Streaks of red and purple wove through the swelling here and there. The damage wasn't old. Gabe reached down and touched the injury. Harris growled, flung his arms across his chest, and shivered. The skin was fever hot. Gabe courteously turned his head, dragged the damp, discolored boxers off the man, and tossed the bedding over him in one fell swoop.

Heading for the door, groans stopped him. "C-c-cold. Help. Help me. Please."

Gabe massaged his forehead. What more could he do?

"H-h-help m-m-me."

Gabe turned. Harris was trembling so much the whole bed shook. He had to do something. Heaving a sigh of resignation, he crossed the room. With volumes of trepidation, he slipped off his shoes, then his vest, which he hung on the doorknob, pulled down the covers, and climbed in. He sidled up next to Harris and put his arms around him, stroking his wet hair. "We can't make a habit of this, Mr. Harris. People will talk." But the stirring in Gabe's groin indicated Mr. Harris might be a most welcome habit.

CHAPTER 5

CHARLIE kept his eyes closed as the hotel manager slid out of bed. He remained motionless, providing no hint he was aware the man tiptoed out of the room until the door latched. Then he kicked off the covers and rolled to the edge of the mattress.

He sat, winced, and slugged down a mouthful of air. His thigh was on fire. He rolled his head over his neck. Cracks and snaps splintered tensed nerves. He turned. The pea coat hung as a reminder of the man who owed him nothing, but had provided Charlie more than the manager would ever know.

Charlie'd nearly lost it out there in the street. A laugh spilled out of him. *Nearly? A nutcase. That's what you are.* And yet, the manager had done for him what only one other man had ever done—worried about... cared about... him. Something writhed in his stomach and crawled upward. Charlie nipped it by bending and picking up his duffle. He opened it and dug around for the bottle of Bufferin. He unscrewed the cap and shook a couple into his mouth, then swallowed them dry.

Time remained an unknown, but if the shade of black behind the curtains of the lone window meant anything, it was late. And with no word from Roger, he still had no idea what he was doing here. He dumped the contents of the duffle on the bed. A clean pair of boxers, socks, jeans, tee, and a flannel shirt, and he was ready to go. He slipped on his boots. At the pea coat, he ran a hand over the wool and smiled. The darn thing hadn't felt so clean in a long time.

He walked to the window and pulled back the curtains. The fire escape was near enough if it came to that. The problem was, he just wasn't quite sure what *that* was. With a bit of luck, he wouldn't need to find out. But he did have some unfinished business.

He closed the door behind him.

GABE hit every other step up the stairs to his apartment.

How could he have fallen asleep? Once Harris's trembling had stopped, he should have left. But he hadn't. He'd stayed there, next to him, reveling in the pleasure of the man in his arms. Now he needed to hurry or he'd miss the train.

He threw some clothes in a valise, then rearranged them to prevent wrinkles. Finished, he dialed the phone. MN 321.

"Whistle Pass Cab."

"Carol—"

"Gabe. I was starting to wonder if you'd call. I'll send Clarence right over. Train's due any minute now."

He bolted down the stairs. The sun yellow cab slid to a stop. Gabe jumped in the back. Clarence whipped a U-turn and sped down the wet street.

"What do you find to do in Chicago, Gabe? I suppose it's exciting and all in the big city, but every weekend?"

Morose, he stared out the window. "Live the life I don't have here."

They arrived at the Milwaukee depot as the passenger train slowed to a stop. Gabe ran into the small wood-framed building and set the correct change on the window counter. The ticket agent handed him a ticket, and Gabe ran out the double doors.

The conductor punched his ticket, and Gabe climbed the steps. Quickly walking through two cars to the Pullman car, he found his seat and tossed his bag onto the overhead luggage rack. Sitting, he stuck his ticket under the metal tab on the wall so the conductor passing through would see his ticket had been punched and not disturb him. He laid his head back on the red leather seat and inhaled the dense combination of diesel and exhaust fumes.

He adjusted his shoulders to ease an inner discomfort. Something was different. The butterflies of anticipation hadn't climbed onboard with him. Excitement should have filled him like a child on Christmas morning. Instead, he felt more like every opened present had been pajamas.

The car jerked, then slowly rolled forward. The air replenished and recycled, cleaning away the residue of the station. Gabe reached up and switched off the reading lamp. Turning, he idly watched the shadowy freight cars in the yards pass by until darkness obscured his view. The rhythmic clickety-clack of steel wheels on steel rails lulled him to a semi-dream state.

Charlie Harris was in his arms once again. But this time, they were both naked.

THE rain had stopped, replaced by a thick paste of damp. Charlie stuffed his hands in the pockets of the pea coat. *Damn it.* Empty. He looked up and down the street, chose the lighted ship's wheel as the most likely target, and began walking. In the next block he could make out "BAR" in green letters under the wheel. He strode through the dank street until he stood under the sign. Through the small window of the wooden door, he could see a few lights were on, so he pulled the door open and walked in.

It took a few seconds for his vision to adjust. Not many people in the place. One at the bar. Two at one of the six tables. The Hamm's clock on the wall answered his question of what time it had gotten to be: ten thirty. The bubbling Wurlitzer stood silent. Just as well. Charlie wasn't in the mood for music. He sat on a stool at the bar. A balding, potbellied man in a soiled white shirt and suspenders walked over to him.

"What can I get you?"

"Pack of Luckies and a bottle of Busch."

The barkeep pulled the cigarette pack from a wall rack and tossed it onto the bar along with a pack of matches. Charlie ripped open one end, tapped out the tip of a cigarette, then pulled it out between his teeth. He folded the matchbook cover behind one match, which he thumbed across the striker, and blew out when he exhaled the first puff.

The bottle of beer appeared in front of him. Charlie set a crumpled dollar on the bar. "Keep it."

The bartender snapped the bill open and closed twice. "To what do I owe the honor? You don't look like Daddy Warbucks. Must want something for this kind of tip."

Charlie looked around again. "Always this quiet on a Friday night? Don't the kids around here cut loose on Main Street?"

"No, and yes. Just not tonight. Weather's too shitty for most folks to come out. Hunters didn't come to town for the same reason. I'm gonna close early if it stays like this. Street punks are all mourning out at the roller rink."

"Mourning? Who died?"

A thin brow rose. "You live in a cave?"

"The hotel."

The bartender curled a lip. "Same difference. Railroader, huh? Been all over the news. That greaser movie star James Dean killed himself in a car wreck."

Charlie nodded knowingly, even though he had no clue who James Dean was. "Where's the roller rink?"

The bartender wiped a cloth across the bar and met Charlie's gaze. "Why? Only kids and punks hang out there. You don't look like either one. But you might look like trouble."

"Me?" Charlie shook his head. "Not me. First time I ever laid over here. Just like to know where the trouble's at so I can avoid it is all. Need my job more than I need a night in the slammer. Speaking of which, what time's the night heat come on? I s'pose like most places the night cop here's the biggest jerk of the bunch."

The man chuckled. "Got that right. Comes on at eleven. If you're buying your drinks over on Fourth Street, you got no problem. They pay him to turn a blind eye to the slots in the basement. But downtown where we run clean businesses, Austin's a hemorrhoid."

"Austin?"

"Phil Austin." The man folded his arms on the bar and leaned over them. "You sure you're not looking for trouble?"

Charlie guzzled the beer and set down the empty bottle. "Never know when you might need a cop. Pays to know who might be coming."

The man pocketed Charlie's dollar. "Name's Captain Tom. I own this place. From now on, you've got a running tab here. Settle up the end of each layover before you leave town." He winked. "And, you ever need an alibi, I'll swear you were here 'til closing, Mr....?"

"Charlie Harris." Charlie slid off the stool.

"One more thing, Charlie."

"What's that?"

"Since you're new and all, and staying at the hotel. Watch your butt around that manager they got there."

Charlie tensed. The hotel manager could be a problem. His staff would know all his comings and goings. "Why? What about him?"

Captain Tom leaned farther over the beer-stained bar and lowered his voice. "He's a butt packer. He may have been born here, but he's one of them queers you hear about, all the same. When he's around, keep your back to the wall."

Charlie relaxed, then tensed up again. The manager wasn't a threat, but he bit back the urge to rip off Captain Tom's mizzenmast and ram it down his throat. "I'll remember you said that." He took a long drag on the cigarette and glared at the bartender through the smoke. "If you don't like *them queers*, why don't you do something about one in your town?"

The man rocked his head back and forth. "Like I said, he was born here. Until we catch him wearing women's clothes or hanging around the grade school, that's the way it is, and the way it stays. You don't mess with one of your own 'til you have reason to. But we ever have reason to, we'll have us a little fun some night."

Charlie snorted his contempt in two lines of smoke that spilled across the bar. "Would you call me a cab?"

"Sure thing. You're a cab." A snicker parted chafed lips, followed by a guffaw. He picked up the phone and laughed into the receiver. "Good one, huh?"

"Yeah. You're a real Red Skelton." He quickly walked outside to avoid breaking a chair over somebody's head.

The cab arrived in less than three minutes.

"Where to?"

"Not going anywhere, really. Would you just drive me past the roller rink so I can see where it is and then drop me at the hotel?"

"You're the boss. Still cost you a quarter, though."

Charlie sat back on the seat, smoking a cigarette, as they cruised the roller rink. Like leather-jacketed roaches, a number of them crawled in and out and over cars. He smiled and took a drag off the Lucky. The red-headed roach was sitting on top of the driver's seat of an aqua Chevy convertible. Large furry dice hung from the mirror.

"Want to stop, or you still want to go to the hotel?" the cab driver asked.

"Hotel's good."

HE STEPPED out of the cab and into the entryway of the hotel. When the cab drove away, Charlie jogged across the street. He walked around the corner and into the alley. As he walked, he studied the second-floor porches. In the third block he found what he wanted—a porch with no stairway.

Charlie slipped out of his coat and stashed it behind a couple of trashcans. He rubbed his hands over a round support pole, then shinnied up to the porch. Grabbing an outer flooring board, he swung himself up to the railing and climbed over it. Not knowing when the cop would come along, he retreated into the shadows and waited.

He figured it to be an hour, somewhere around midnight, when the squad appeared in the alley. The spotlight's beam washed over doorways and stairways, but not the porch Charlie was on. Charlie smiled. The copper wasn't concerned about upper levels with no exposed way to get to them.

When the squad passed and entered the next block's alley, Charlie scooted down the pole and retrieved his coat. He walked back to the hotel and up the stairs to his room. After unlocking the door, he swung it open and then stood dead still in the doorway.

The man stretched out on his bed, illuminated by the bulb under the butterfly shade of the lamp on the nightstand, didn't flash the smile displayed on the campaign poster. In fact, he didn't appear anywhere even close to smiling. The green eyes heated to a color nearing ruby. "What are you doing in Whistle Pass, Charlie?"

Charlie closed the door behind him. Whatever sliver of hope he'd held in his heart was fading fast with the man's less than pleased scowl. "Nice to see you too, Roger."

CHAPTER 6

THE train's final stop—Chicago's Union Station.

In the concrete cavern, the ceiling black from the era of coal-burning steam engines, Gabe walked along the cement floor, dodging pillars and people in more of a hurry than he was. He pulled open a glass door and made a left through the primary orifice of space. Newspaper hawkers shouted the headlines. Their voices echoed under the domed ceiling and cascaded around the wide array of passengers ignoring them. "James Dean dead. Read all about it. Get your paper here!" Public address speakers yawned destinations. "Last call for Omaha. Gate 14."

He opened another door and walked outside. This ceiling of concrete protected a circular driveway filled with taxis hungry for a fare. Exhaust fumes choked him, clung to his clothing as if living denizens of a world he wasn't welcome in. A man in a burgundy waistcoat and black cap asked, "Cab, sir?"

"Evanston. Botanic Inn," Gabe said.

The man put a silver whistle to his lips and blasted three loud bursts of noise. A green cab jumped out of line and pulled in front of him. The man in the waistcoat opened the back door and Gabe climbed in. "Botanic Inn," the man told the driver.

The driver slammed down a metal lever on the fare box and pulled out of the alcove into the city's traffic. Gabe glanced at the box to ensure the count didn't begin any higher than the thirty-five cents for a single passenger, then closed his eyes to the lights and inhabitants in this concrete ant farm.

"Botanic Inn."

Gabe batted his eyelids and groaned. He'd fallen asleep. A doorman in top hat and tails opened the door.

The driver turned and put his arm over the seat. "That'll be $2.35. Make it $2.50?"

Gabe shoved some bills into the expectant hand. "Make it three skins. I'm not paying for it." He slid out of the cab.

"Thank you, sir. Thank you indeed."

Gabe stuffed a lone dollar into the gloved hand of the doorman as he entered the hotel lobby thick with potted plants on a mosaic floor, the scent of lilac drifting from one fan's blades to the next and back again. Minimum wage had just gone up to a buck an hour, and for the sake of appearances, it was essential he tip accordingly.

"Mr. Simons!" the desk clerk called out. "So good to see you again, sir. Arthur, take Mr. Simons's bag for him."

A red-uniformed bellhop scurried to the desk, where the clerk handed him a key. Gabe handed over the valise.

"Your regular room is all ready for you, Mr. Simons. If there's anything we can do for you, please, do not hesitate to call."

"Thank you, Joseph, I will." Gabe dutifully followed the bellhop to the elevator. A colored woman slid the brass-coated door closed and pushed the button for the sixth floor.

It never ceased to amaze Gabe how in a hotel with the most modern of elevators, no longer requiring an operator, luxury dictated the operator remain, if to do nothing more than relieve the passenger of the inconvenience of pushing a button. The door opened to a maroon deco runner traversing the length of the hallway. Gabe trailed the bellhop to 623 at the end of the hall, next to a stairway. The bellhop swung the door open and stood back to allow Gabe to enter first.

"Where would you like your bag, sir?"

"Just put it on the dresser." Gabe handed over a dollar and sat on the soft quilts overlaying the bed. He ran his feet over the plush carpet and stared at the sheen of the glossy white walls. The door closed and the phone rang. He leaned over and picked up the receiver on the nightstand. "Yes?"

"Anthony! We're in the bar. Get dressed. There's someone special I want you to meet."

We? He sighed. "Of course." He dropped the receiver onto the cradle. "We."

Gabe emptied his lungs in a long, slow stream and stood. He slipped out of his coat, then his shirt, and went to the bathroom, resplendent with its brass fixtures and porcelain knobs. The man in the mirror reflected imperfection. Not a wrinkle, not a roll of fat anywhere. A toned, sleek body. But the image had no soul, no strength of character. That had all washed away a long time ago. He pulled up the brass handle to close off the sink's drain and turned on the hot water. Steam quickly cloaked the wall-length mirror.

With a fingertip he outlined the distorted figure. Then he drew in a zipper-shaped line between the abdomen and ribcage. A dot next beneath the right breast, another just below the right shoulder, and one more left center breast. He stood back and appraised his handiwork.

"How did you survive? What is there within you that refused to die?" He placed a hand over the center of the chest, over Charlie Harris's heart. "I really want to know."

He added some cold to the sink full of hot water, rubbed soap on a washcloth, and scrubbed his body. After, he rinsed and dried his skin.

At the closet he opened the door and selected a suit. Navy pinstripe. The other end held the shirts. A powder blue one would go well with the wool suit. He left his choice of attire on the hangers and sat on the bed. Why had he allowed this to happen?

The courtship had been the answer to his prayers. Private dinners in fine restaurants, surrounded by Chicago's nobility. Dancing in private clubs. Gabe had quickly learned that if a wallet was fat enough, same-sex partners were almost acceptable in some circles. Then came the first offering of cash. A courtesy. Merely a stipend to cover his travel expenses. Slowly, the dinners reduced to room service. The dancing, strictly between the sheets. The amount of money in the envelope increased. Now on the rare occasion when they ventured out on the town, Gabe was more bauble than companion.

Ring, ring. Ring, ring.

He glanced at the phone.

Ring, ring.

He sucked in his lips.

Ring, ring.

He placed a hand over the receiver.

Ring, ring.

Damn you, Gabriel. He picked up the phone. "Yes?"

"Will you hurry up? My friend has somewhere to be later." A click signaled the conversation had ended.

Fingertips over his torso, between abdomen and ribcage, he pondered Charlie Harris. Why was the man in Whistle Pass? Who was Harris's keeper? Was he nothing more than a kept man too? Or was he trouble for hire? Or just trouble? The dates and money for the room reservation had arrived special delivery. Totally impersonal, completely discreet. But Harris had asked about the mayor, oblivious to Roger Black's status in the community. If Black had sent for him, wouldn't Harris know something about the man he'd traveled to see?

Curious.

Harris was an unknown. An anomaly. He didn't appear to have two nickels to rub together, and didn't seem to care. There was nothing he could offer in the way of the lifestyle Gabe wanted. The man probably wasn't interested in men. Not to mention the symptoms of shellshock indicating he might be insane. But Gabe couldn't get him out of his mind.

He stood and pulled the clothing from the closet.

THEY sat at a corner table in the Orchid Room, deemed such by a wall mural. Two men graying at the temples, the third much younger. Younger than Gabe's twenty-four, even. The three men stood as he approached.

"Anthony, this is Mark. Isn't he just the most gorgeous thing you ever did see? He's a student at the university."

The blond young man smiled. Gabe shook the fingers of the extended hand, wondering what *Mark's* real name might be. Not that it mattered. Introductions apparently concluded, they sat. An envelope found its way under the table onto his lap. But not from his host.

His host was lost in Mark's blue eyes. Gabe turned to the bulbous man reeking of bacon fat to his left.

"Two hundred for the weekend, right?" floated to his ears on a carpet of belched garlic.

"Excuse me?" A sweat of indignation oozed from Gabe's pores. "What do you think I am?"

The man leaned over to him. A hand clamped down on Gabe's knee. "I know what you are. I don't have all night. Let's go up to your room and find out if those lips are worth the price." The pressure on Gabe's knee increased. The face soured, the voice graveled to threat. "They better be."

Heat washed over Gabe in broken waves. Anger baked his skin. He just wasn't sure who he was mad at—the men at the table... or himself. "You asshole," he muttered.

"Anthony, sit down. You're causing a scene."

Gabe looked around. A few heads at other tables lowered their gaze. He *was* standing. Hadn't done it knowingly. But it was as good a position as any. "Asshole." He smiled. "Asshole!" he shouted. "Asshole, asshole, asshole!"

"Sit down, you little...."

Gabe scorned the pocked face. "Little what? Queer? I *am* a queer." He thrust out his arms and posed on his invisible cross. "Ladies and gentlemen! I... am a queer!" He lowered his arms to his sides.

"And so are these men, but they don't have the guts to admit it." Mark jumped to his feet and ran out of the room. Gabe followed him with his eyes, chuckling. He tore the pinstripe suit coat off and laid it over the back of the chair. "This isn't mine." He kicked off his shoes. "Or these."

A woman at a neighboring table looked up at him. "That's correct, madam. I'm also a whore." He cocked his head slightly. The woman was much, much younger than the man accompanying her. "Are you, by chance?" Her hands went to her face. The man at her table bolted on the same escape route Mark had taken. "We should start a union."

"Mr. Simons. I must insist you leave. Right now!"

From under his brows, Gabe looked at the desk clerk. "I was just leaving anyway." He unbuttoned the shirt and removed it. Dropping it to the floor, he sang, "Not mine." As he walked, he unbuckled the leather belt, unbuttoned the trousers, then unzipped them. At the door, he let the pants fall to his ankles. He stepped out of them and fumbled with the waistband of his boxers. "Let's all be glad these *do* belong to me."

"Oh, what the hell." He turned to the tabled stares. "I got paid a hundred a night for this." He pushed down the boxers. "So, what do you think? Too much for too little? Or should I have demanded more?"

Women screamed and gasped. Men covered ladies' faces. One woman pushed her gallant escort's hand away and smiled appreciatively.

Gabe glowed and bowed. "Thank you, madam."

"*Mr. Simons!*" The clerk grabbed his arm.

Gabe pulled the boxers in place. Shoulders proudly back, he strode into the lobby, inhaling the wonderful lilac fragrance for the last time. A bellhop handed him the clothes he had worn in and his valise. "Thank you. I'm afraid I am a bit short on cash to tip you, my good man."

"Out. Out!"

Gabe ignored the desk clerk and headed for the door held open by the uniformed doorman. A taxi sat waiting. He climbed into the backseat and dug $2.35 from the trousers in his hands. "Sorry. No tip this trip."

The cab sped down the street. Gabe dressed, wondering all the while what Charlie Harris would have done in this situation.

CHAPTER 7

THE edge of the mattress scrunched under Roger's weight when he sat upright. "What are you doing here, Charlie?"

Charlie, more confused than ever, took off his coat and hung it on the back of the door. There being no chairs in the room, he sat a foot away from Roger, adding a physical void to the emotional one between them. He pulled over the duffle and rooted out the telegram.

Roger read the message, turned the paper over and back again. "I didn't send this."

Charlie's heart sank. He'd hoped, no matter how faint the chance might be, Roger'd decided he had to have him in his life. "But you're the only person who ever said 'Need you' to me. Unless you told somebody about us?" The thought of Roger nonchalantly gossiping over coffee and donuts about what they'd shared filleted his guts. "You didn't, did you?"

The man's head snapped around to glare at Charlie. "Are you nuts? Do you know what something like that would do to my political career? Christ. If anybody ever found out...."

Charlie put his hand over his mouth and looked at the ceiling. He'd become the dirty little secret in a budding politician's past. What had been beautiful and clean was now ugly and mired in mud, a political opponent's fodder.

A hand kneaded his shoulder. He pulled away and stood.

"I didn't mean it like that. I'm sorry."

"I want you to leave, Roger. I need to pack. There's no reason for me to hang around here." He pivoted on a heel to face the man. "And, don't worry. I'll take your embarrassment to the grave. Now, please, get out." He didn't know if he wanted to scream, curse, cry, or break something. Most likely, all the above.

Roger didn't move. "Sit down, Charlie. We have to talk."

"No. Get out."

Roger patted the covers. "Don't you see? Somebody knows, and I have to find out who. Now I *do* need you. I need your help."

Charlie shook his head. "Not my problem."

"You might want to consider this, Charlie. I had no idea where to find you, even if I'd wanted to. But whoever sent the telegram did. There's more to this. Give me a few minutes. Please? Sit down and listen to what I have to say."

Before Charlie decided either way, there was one question that needed answering. "Did you send a cop to beat the crap out of me?"

The smirk on Roger's face didn't set well.

"Austin." He shook his head. "No. I didn't. But he would have done it thinking he was protecting me."

"Protecting you? From what?"

"From whoever's been sending me death threats. I told you there's more. Will you please sit and listen?"

Wanting Roger gone was one thing—dead, quite another. Charlie plopped down next to him. "So, talk."

"This year the Atomic Energy Commission began a program funding nuclear power plants between government and industry." His eyes lit up like headlights. "We can have one of the first plants here, Charlie. Right here in Whistle Pass. History, Charlie. Can you imagine? This town would be famous."

"Or infamous. What if the damn thing blows up? You'd be a hole in the ground."

Roger frowned. "That's the kind of caveman mentality I've been dealing with around here. It's why I'm running for state office, so I can make this happen."

"But you're getting death threats. I take it some of the local *cavemen* aren't too thrilled. How do you think you can win if the people don't support what you're doing?"

The frown slid to a sly grin. "Because this is the smallest county in the district, and I'm a big hit in the other ones where the plant won't be located. The service provider we're negotiating with has agreed to reduce the cost of electricity to all the county users. Once the people learn what a boon the plant is, they'll take pride in what I'm doing for them."

Charlie scoffed. "Uh-huh." He shifted his weight a little. "What is it you think I can do for you?"

"Nobody knows you here. All I'm asking is for you to mingle and keep your eyes and ears open. If you come up with something, let me know. That's it. That's all. I'll turn it over to the police once we have a lead to follow, and you can go back to wherever it is you came from."

Charlie squeezed a wince of doubt. "Aren't you forgetting about whoever sent the telegram? And, by the way, paid for this room?"

Roger didn't miss a beat. "It has to be the same people, Charlie. They want to destroy me. We just have to find them first." He reached over and grabbed Charlie's hand. He pulled it to his lips. "We had something special once. If I ever meant anything to you, please help me now."

Fury roiled inside him. Charlie jerked out of his grasp. "You're a real piece of work, Roger. No doubt, you'll be governor someday."

The candidate simply smiled. "That's the plan."

He wanted to pack his bag and go, but the temptation of finding out who'd jumped him in the hall, and why, set his tongue scrubbing the back of his teeth while he considered sticking around. Finally he said, "Room's paid for anyway. I'll give it a shot for a couple days."

Roger put a hand on his shoulder and stood. "Thank you, Charlie. I'll owe you. You ever need anything, just ask. It's yours."

He *needed* the man he'd fallen in love with. But it didn't look like that possibility—or the man—existed.

Roger walked to the door, then paused, hand on the knob. "You don't still have that other picture the war correspondent took, do you?"

"Nah. Burned it years ago."

"Good." He opened the door. "Couldn't afford to have something like that surfacing now." The click of the latch echoed in the empty part of Charlie's heart once filled by Roger.

He reached in the duffle and pulled out a pocket-sized leather folder. Separating the dried and cracked cover, he looked at the weathered photo. Two men, naked to the waist, embracing and lost in an impassioned kiss. Charlie's back had been to the camera they didn't know was there. The face so readily identifiable was the candidate for state representative himself.

The correspondent had given the picture to Charlie in the hospital. Said he'd planned to publish it, but given the ambush and what Charlie had done to save the few who lived that late afternoon, he'd decided the affair was a story the folks back home didn't need to read yet.

Charlie rubbed a thumb on his chin. Roger'd said he didn't send the telegram, but he sure thought to ask about the photo quick enough. Might be worth hanging on to a while longer until he figured out what was going on. But the picture needed to be in a safe place, and this room wasn't safe. There might be a haven for it, though. He stuck the folder and photograph inside the pillowcase and stretched out, laying his head on the pillow. For now, he'd sleep on it.

MORTARS exploded. Men screamed.

Charlie whirled, looking for where the attack would come from. "Stay low! Stay—"

He cracked open an eyelid. Thunder rattled the window frame. Rain pelted the glass. The hotel room. "Just a storm," he heaved out in a breath. Not bothering to change clothes, he slipped on his pea coat. He retrieved the folder from the pillowcase and stuck it in a pocket.

THE restaurant wasn't large. On the left side was a wall-length wooden counter and register stand. Glass-doored cabinets displayed a variety of glasses and cups. Blue seat covers on chrome pedestals bellied customers up to the soda bar. Against the wall were tables for two. Down the length of the center of the room were similar tables with four blue chairs with beige backs positioned at each side. The wall by the tables was dark blue tile to shoulder height, then yellow wallpaper to a white ceiling stained orange by tobacco smoke.

The smell of cigarettes and cigars crawled up Charlie's nose before the bacon, eggs, potatoes, and fresh coffee settled in.

A middle-aged woman with dark hair wound in a coil on top of her head, wearing a pale blue dress, yellow apron, and sneakers zipped past him, coffeepot in hand. "Set yourself anywhere you can, doll. We'll find you."

He scanned the tables but didn't see an empty chair. Two men in overalls and gray polka dot caps rose from a wall table. They picked up metal lunch pails and lanterns and headed for the register. Charlie grabbed a seat.

A younger version of the first woman grabbed up the empty plates, then returned with a wet rag and swabbed down the table. She produced a pad and pencil from her apron. "What's buzzin, cuzzin?"

Charlie leaned back and looked at her, unsure what she meant.

Her left nostril flared, and her tone softened. "What'll you have, sugar?"

"Coffee. Black."

"Coming up." She faded into the crowd of men eating, smoking, and talking. The din of unintelligible conversations and clinks of silverware on plates only served to annoy him. She reappeared with a mug of brew. "Just leave a dime on the table. Need anything, holler out." She skittered away to other customers.

Charlie pulled out the pack of Luckies, lit one, and rolled the paper's ash off in a small glass ashtray. He exhaled over the top of the steaming coffee.

"Good morning, Gabe. Full house. Want us to bring over something instead of waiting for a seat?" a woman's voice called out over the ball of jagged sound.

Charlie looked over the top of the mug. The hotel manager stood in the doorway. *Gabe.* Hadn't heard his name mentioned before. He raised the mug and moved it slowly back and forth. The manager's eyes shifted to his right. Charlie motioned to the empty chair. Gabe nodded and walked over.

"Welcome to join me." Charlie took another drag off the cigarette and blew it over the top of the coffee before taking a cautious sip. It was hot, but good.

"Want me to take your coat? I'll put it in the back with ours." The offer came from the younger waitress.

Gabe unbuttoned and slipped off the wool knee-length black coat and draped it over her extended arm. He carefully removed his hat with both hands, lifting it straight upward, then handed her the fedora as well. The dark blue shirt appeared pressed and starched.

"Usual?"

He patted the sides of his hair. "Yes. Thank you, Cathy." She darted off. Gabe pulled out the chair and sat, straight and proper. A whiff of Aqua Velva sat with him. "Thank you, Mr. Harris."

Charlie blew out another cloud of smoke. "Not a problem. Figured I owed you breakfast, at least, for what I put you through in my room." He watched the man carefully over the top of the mug he was hiding behind.

Gabe's cheeks flushed rose. A hand went up to the hair and patted the top. Charlie quirked a corner of his mouth. The man's sculpted black hair looked like a magazine ad for barbers. So did the face, shaved so not a hair dared show a tip. There wasn't any visible nose hair either. *What? You trim that too?* The gaze of the pale gray eyes under perfect brows lowered to the table. Gabe busied himself adjusting the salt and pepper to an equidistance from the chrome napkin holder. Apparently satisfied with the placement, he placed his hands in his lap.

"You don't have to buy me breakfast."

Charlie swallowed another swig. "Want to."

"No, I mean, breakfast comes with the job." The cheeks flashed crimson. "The Larson family owns this place too. I get breakfast for free."

"Really? Nice job." He hit the cigarette again and blew the smoke over Gabe's hair. The manager reached up and smoothed the hairs that hadn't so much as jostled.

"You always do that?"

Gabe looked up. "Do what?"

"Check your hair."

The cheeks went directly to maroon.

"You're not wearing your vest or a tie. Off today?"

Gabe fidgeted in his seat. "I have weekends free. Normally I spend them out of town, but my plans changed."

Charlie gulped down the coffee and set the empty mug on the table. Time to go for broke. If he had a shot at trusting anyone in this town, it would be the hotel manager living a life of secrets. "I need a favor."

The manager's left eye twitched.

Charlie pulled the leather photo protector from his coat pocket and set it on the table. "I'd appreciate it if you'd put this someplace safe until I ask for it back."

Gabe stared at the object but didn't make a move to reach for it, so Charlie pushed the pocket-sized parcel of dynamite toward him. "Take a look. It won't bite." *Much.*

The man picked it up and peeled open the leather cover. His jaw nearly fell into his lap.

Charlie stood and dropped a dime on the table. It spun and rolled, then fell still. He looked down at Roosevelt's face. "Heads. She wins." He tossed another dime, a tip for the waitress, onto the table, then looked at Gabe as he retrieved the tossed coin. "Yeah. It's who you think it is." He took a step forward and leaned over to Gabe's ear. "And the one with his back to the camera is me. Appears you and me have something in common. Call me Charlie."

He walked out the door into the morning molasses of fog.

CHAPTER 8

LOGIC was a hula hoop he couldn't get hold of circling his brain. Gabe snuck another peek at the photo, then slapped the cover closed, looking around the room for prying eyes. He concentrated and forced his fear-paralyzed lungs to work. There were movies about pictures like this. People got killed because of pictures like this.

Alfred Hitchcock would kill a dozen people over a picture like this.

He bolted out the door. A shadow faded into the gray soup. Gabe ran after and around it.

"Charlie. Do you know what this is?" he asked, holding up the folder. He saw his trembling hand, grabbed it with the other. Now both hands shook.

Charlie grinned. Gabe sighed. The man had a great grin. "Yeah. I was there. I know exactly what it is. It's a picture of two men who were in love." His voice lowered. "And I think somebody wants to get their hands on it. That's why I gave it to you."

Gabe clamped his knees together and shifted his weight from one foot to the other. He really needed to pee. Fear filled bladders too damn fast. *Somebody wants it*? The trembling moved into his empty stomach. "Why do you think somebody knows about this picture? Have you told anyone about it?"

A figure broke through the curtains of mist, hurrying past. Gabe grabbed Charlie's lapel and pulled him into a doorway. "Did something happen?" *Charlie's leg*. The fresh bruises. He held up the photo binder. "Did you get that injury on your thigh because of this?"

Charlie's hands pushed Gabe's down. His bushy brows dipped and converged into a singular line of forestry. "Would you mind putting that away somewhere? I didn't give it to you to show everybody on the street."

Gabe's face burned his embarrassment. "Sorry." He slipped the packet into his back pocket, behind his wallet.

Charlie's shoulders sank in visible relief. "No. That night cop, Austin, paid me a visit. Thought I might be a threat to the mayor."

Gabe swallowed hard. "Are you?" *What are you doing? Give him the picture back and get as far away from this man as you can.*

Charlie turned slightly and spoke over his shoulder. "Do you have a car?"

"No." Gabe chewed his lip. *Walk away. Now!* But his tongue wasn't listening to his brain. "I can get a car." *Oh, Lord. Now you've done it.*

"Meet me around the corner of the hotel at ten tonight." Charlie stepped out of the doorway and disappeared into the fog.

Gabe quickly pulled a key out of his pocket, went to the next door on the block and unlocked it. He ran all the way up the stairs, then unlocked the door to his apartment.

Standing in the center of the room, he tapped the leather folder against his temple. "Where do I put you?" He scanned an immaculately smoothed bed, the dust-free veneer dresser, the closet, the radiator's metal lace cover. Too easy. Anyone really looking would find the picture. So, where? He leaned his head back and stared at the ceiling, then at the ceiling molding. He smiled.

With one foot on the dresser and one on the bed's burled walnut headboard, his fingertips rocked a piece of molding nailed into the plaster wall. Little by little it loosened until a space just large enough revealed itself. He slid the photo and cover behind it, slapped the board back in place, and then ran down the stairs.

Breakfast was waiting. But he'd have to send it back. What he needed most was to vomit.

CHARLIE walked into the newsstand. A round soda table with two iron stools stood vacant next to the window, affording him a view of the barely visible doors to city hall immediately across the street. On the table rested a newspaper. He checked the date. Three days old. But the title was *The Weekly Whistle*, so he figured it was the latest edition.

"Coffee?" the man behind the counter asked.

"Yeah. Black." He read the headline and shivered.

The man set a mug of brew in front of him. "Yes, sir. Iowa knows how to handle them damn homosexuals. If the rest of this country'd follow suit, the world would be a safer place. You want anything else? Got some frosted donuts."

Charlie pulled his fingertips over his face, stretching his skin as he did. "No. I'm good." The man shuffled away, and Charlie stared at the headline: "Iowa Commits 29 Homosexuals to Mental Asylums." He shook out a Lucky and lit up. He exhaled and refilled his lungs. Smoke leaked from his nostrils. *Yeah. Lock up all the insane Gabes and Charlies, and the world will be safe for the fine, upstanding citizens like Roger Black.*

He clenched the cigarette between his teeth and combed back his hair with his fingers. In the northern forests of Wisconsin, men looked the other way. As long as each bunk only had one body on it at night, nobody questioned what happened out of sight behind a tree.

He sipped at the coffee for a while, making it last longer than he usually would. Time dragged into two more cigarettes. The supply low, he called out, "Can I get a pack of Lucky Strikes?"

The pack hit the table as the doors to city hall opened. But the uniformed cop walking out plucked the last of a cigarette from his lips and chucked it into the street. *No ceegar, Charlie boy.* He'd have to try later when the shift changed. His bet was that one of the city cops smoked Red Dot cigars. "What do I owe you?"

"Thirty-five cents with the smokes."

Charlie pinched open a red rubber coin holder and counted out the correct change, then tossed a dime on the table. It spun and rolled before settling torch side up. "Tails, you lose."

The man squinted. "What'd I lose?"

Charlie picked up the dime and put it back in his pocket. "Your tip." He pushed open the door and walked out to the sidewalk. Hands in his pockets, he inhaled the smell of the river under the column of smoke rising from the cigarette in his mouth and turned toward the water.

He ambled along the bank, idly watching the green water lap at wave-smoothed rocks. Finding an iron bench with wood slats, he sat. He ran his hand across the wood, shaving off a few featherings of white paint. The cigarette at its end, he pinched out the final drag and flicked the butt into the river. Water tore at the paper until tobacco spilled out.

Charlie closed his eyes, laid his head back, and wondered what a man as handsome as Gabe was doing in a town that obviously had no use for him. He coughed out a single note chuckle. *Handsome*. It had been a long time since he'd thought of a man as handsome; since... Roger.

A rush of heat stirred his groin. He shifted his hips to counter the movement. Apparently his eyes weren't the only part of him that found Gabe attractive.

GABE donned his coat and hat and took a step toward the door of the restaurant. Realization stopped him cold. Austin had beat Charlie. But how had Austin known he was at the hotel? Maybe he'd seen him arrive.

"Cathy, would you call me a cab?"

"Sure, Gabe."

He turned up his collar and went outside to wait. Maybe Austin had stumbled upon Charlie. But maybe not. There was one man who sure as hell had known when Charlie Harris arrived.

GABE exited the cab and grabbed the sidewalk's iron pipe handrail. Little flashes of white swirled in a whirlpool of discomfort and insecurity. He closed his eyes, hoping the moment of height vertigo would pass quickly. He detested coming to this part of town, constructed in layers onto the side of the river bluff—houses, then a street on the next level with stairs leading down, or up, depending on one's perspective, a row of houses, pavement, and so on to the crest many yards and crooked stairs above him. Trees grew at angles, only to curve sharply toward the sun, which still wasn't visible through the fog. Nor was the river far below.

Thus his uneasiness. When he could see the downtown below, know where he'd stop if he fell, the vertigo tended to be a dull throb in his temples. He wasn't so much afraid of heights as he was the fall without end.

The whirlpool drained. The flashes reduced to occasional silver darts thrown at a target behind his eyeballs. He opened his eyes and slowly made his way, one cautious step at a time, down the slick wooden stairs to the wood-frame bungalow painted yellow with green trim.

He knocked on the door and scraped his shoes over the rubber mat. A shrill *yip, yip, yip*, acknowledged his presence. The door opened. The old man held the yapping brown and white Chihuahua in his arms.

"Morning, Edgar. May I come in?"

Edgar clamped fingers over the dog's mouth and kissed the snout. "See? It's just Gabe. Now hush, Muffin." He looked at Gabe and stepped back. "Come on in. Muffin will be a good girl." A turned cheek nuzzled the dog. "Won't you, baby?"

A corner of Gabe's mouth curled. When Edgar's wife died, Muffin had gotten the man through the depression that nearly took his life. God knew what would happen to the man if something happened to the dog. Gabe closed the door behind him.

The dampness in his nostrils was quickly replaced by the dry heat of radiators and the bite of whiskey-laden air… and dog piss. Edgar never drank on the job, that Gabe knew of, but at home was quite a different situation altogether.

"You want to sit? I'll clear you a spot."

Gabe glanced at the tattered couch littered with piles of newspapers and *National Geographic*. "No thanks. I'll just be a minute."

Edgar staggered to a threadbare armchair in a corner of the small room. The dog lay down in his lap with an eye trained on Gabe. Edgar picked up a short glass with a trace of gold liquid in the bottom, downed it, then set the empty glass next to a framed photo of his deceased wife on the round table of the floor lamp. "What can I do for you?" He reached to the floor, picked up a bottle, and refilled the glass to the brim.

Gabe stuck his hands in his coat pockets, rubbing his knuckles with his thumbs. "You called the night cop, Phil Austin, when Charlie Harris checked in." He took a deep breath of the rank air, fighting back a twinge of nausea. "I'd like to know why."

Edgar lifted the glass and sipped the whiskey from the rim before responding. "No secret. Austin always wants to know when somebody strange checks in. You know, somebody alone, not a tourist, and not working for the railroad."

Gabe's ass puckered. He hadn't considered the prospect of every visitor to the city getting the crap beat out of them. At least Austin was apparently selective in who he tortured.

The old man set the glass down again. His hand went to his face; thumb and index finger massaged his eyes. Then he drew the hand downward, pulling his haggard features with it until the hand slipped off the end of his chin. "But I swear I didn't call the police chief." Red-rimmed eyes looked up at Gabe. "I swear. You gotta believe me. I didn't have anything to do with that." He guzzled half the contents of the glass.

"Police chief? *Our* police chief?" A flush of dread surged through him. Sweat beaded under his hat brim. He tugged the fedora off and wiped the droplets from his forehead. Fallen strands of his sculpted hair tickled the top of his ear, but he ignored them. He nervously turned the hat in his hands. Police Chief Howard Perkins was nobody to tangle with.

Edgar's head jerked up and down. "Yeah."

"Anything to do with what? What else happened you didn't tell me about?"

"He showed up in the lobby a half hour before the bus arrived and went upstairs when Harris checked in. A few minutes later he ran downstairs and out the door." A liver-spotted hand tipped back another gulp of whiskey. "If I had to say, I'd say when he ran by me he looked like he'd gotten the snot beat out of him."

Gabe placed the hat back on his head and scrubbed his face with his palms. Charlie'd whupped the police chief but had let Austin decorate his thigh. *Why?* He lowered his hands. "Keep this to yourself, Edgar. Okay?"

The old man gazed at him under low eyelids. "Like I want that son of a bitch Perkins kicking in my door some night? I'm not a kid anymore. I might have been able to go a few rounds with him back in the day, but that was a long time ago." He took a slow drink and set the empty glass on the table. He closed his eyes, laying his head on the back of the chair. A pensive voice muttered, "A long time ago."

Gabe turned and opened the door.

"Gabe." The voice was weak and broken.

"Yes, Edgar?" he asked without looking behind him.

"I'm old and a drunk. But this old gandy dancer still knows when something's not right. You were one of the few who came to Doris's funeral. You need anything, me and Muffin, we'll do what we can."

He nodded and stepped into the doorway. "Thanks."

The voice on the edge of stupor slurred, "If all the queers were like you, maybe it'd be okay."

Gabe closed the door and cringed. *Christ. How many other people know?*

The tops of buildings on Main Street poked through holes in the gray blanket. The fog had lifted to a degree. He crept along the sidewalk, squeezing the handrail as he made his way down the bluff, hand over trembling hand.

Filled with regret that he hadn't asked the cab to wait, Gabe could only wince, gulp, and take the first step into the fog below.

CHARLIE rubbed his eyes and stood. He guessed the time to be somewhere around noon. A sandwich and nap were on the agenda, right after a stop at the hardware store for a set of doorknobs. Too many people seemed to have keys to his hotel room.

Chapter 9

TING ting ting ting ting.

Charlie rolled over and slapped the button on the wind-up alarm clock he'd bought along with the new lock he'd install later. Nine thirty. Pain twisted up from his thigh, and he clamped his eyes shut. "Damn it."

He limped his way to the bathroom and massaged the wound with cold water. The skin was nearly as hard as the sink. The cold numbed the pain enough that he could flex his knee a little, so he slunk back to his room to dress. The Bufferin bottle had four tablets left—he swallowed the bunch dry.

Charlie donned jeans, tee, and flannel shirt. The right boot went on easily. The left, not so much. His leg wouldn't bend enough for him to tie the laces. Pea coat over his arm, he took the elevator to the lobby.

A few men sat on the couches, lunch pails and lanterns at their feet. "Gonna go have me a few drinks. Saturday night in the big city. Yeehaw," Charlie said loud enough everyone should hear. A few pairs of eyes glanced up at him. *That'll do it.*

Outside, the chill nipped at his cheeks, but, fog gone, the night was clear. Two cars raced past, jockeying for the lead. Engines whined. Mufflers rattled. Burnt exhaust filled Charlie's nose. Three blocks south, a horde of leather and high school-jacketed roaches cheered the winner screaming past around the curve out of downtown and out of sight. The door to city hall flew open. Roaches and cars scattered. The cop jumped into the big-finned Chevy and laid rubber.

Charlie smirked at what had to be a Saturday night ritual and rounded the corner of the hotel. A car's headlights blinked on, then off. The green car's chrome hood ornament was a helmeted, mustachioed Spaniard. Gabe leaned over and opened the front passenger door. Charlie sat, closing the door when his legs were inside. The downtown's sound muted. His sinuses filled with Gabe's Aqua Velva aftershave.

Charlie looked around at the cloth seats, the ivory-colored steering wheel, the chrome door handles and window cranks, and the carpeting. "Nice wheels. You jack it?" He dug the pack of Luckies from a pocket, then tossed the pea coat onto the backseat. He flicked his wrist to pop the end of a cigarette out, but Gabe's hand on his stopped him. The skin was warm, the touch soft but firm, and Charlie's body went rigid.

"No, I didn't steal it. I borrowed it from the used car dealer. Told him I wanted to test drive it for the weekend. And... I promised him I wouldn't smoke in it."

In no hurry for Gabe to remove the hand from his, Charlie leaned over to the pack and bit down on a cigarette tip. "You're not. I am."

Gabe's free hand wrapped around Charlie's fingers, clutching the pack of smokes. "Please." The voice was whisper gentle. Charlie's nipples hardened at the tone, soft as a tongue on his throat. "I promised."

Charlie's mouth dried. He tried to squeeze saliva to his gums and lips. Had it been so long a man's touch could make him react this way? Or was it this man? This hotel manager he had nothing in common with and nothing to offer. He blinked, jerked his hand out of Gabe's, and looked out the side window. "Okay." His voice cracked. He swallowed a ball of dust. "I won't smoke."

A key clicked in the ignition, and the engine revved to life. "Thank you. Where do you want to go?"

"Cruise up and down the side and back streets. We're looking for an aqua Chevy convertible."

Gabe shot him a side-glance. "Johnny Upton's car? What for?"

"I'm betting he'll break into my room while I'm out and the cops are in the station changing shifts. Unless he's got a key." He swiveled in the seat and fixed his gaze on the manager. "Everybody else in this town seems to have a key, maybe he does too."

GEARS ground their inability to comply with the driver's demand. Gabe's ears went straight to broil.

"Don't you have to push in the clutch first?"

"It's been a while since I've driven anything. Okay?" He depressed the clutch, shifted into reverse, and eased off the pedal as he backed out of the parking space. He stepped on the clutch pedal again, slid the lever into first, and headed up the street. "Why would Johnny break into your room? He's pure trouble, but he's more the type to burglarize liquor stores and empty tourist cabins."

"The picture. Johnny was part of a welcoming committee when I checked in to your hotel. They had to be after something. That picture's the only thing I can think of anybody would want."

Gabe's stomach churned acid up his throat. "Was one of them a man who'd been in the lobby?"

A rustle on the seat as Charlie turned. His brow dipped; his voice growled. "Red Dot cigar smoker. I take it you know him?"

Shit. "Yes. Our police chief, Howard Perkins. Charlie, he's nobody to fool with. Rumor is, there's more than a couple bodies on the bottom of the river."

"And you people let him get away with murder? Nobody's tried to stop him?"

"They weren't locals. Chicago, I heard tell. Probably gangsters. Who knows who the people really are that come out here?"

A ruptured laugh erupted out of Charlie. "Rumors? Stories over beer? Howard Perkins is a killer because you heard it from somebody who heard from somebody who heard it? You buzzin cuzzins do anything except run your motor mouths around here?"

Gabe compressed his face to a befuddled mass. "Buzzin cuzzins?"

"The waitress at the restaurant called me one."

Gabe laughed. "No. 'What's buzzin cuzzin' is slang for 'what's new'. A greeting. Where you been, Charlie? You a fream?" His chest bounced under his laughter. Charlie's eyes flamed straight through the jocularity. Gabe stopped laughing.

"Watch what you call me," he snarled. "You aren't any different than I am. Just a different hiding place, is all. There! There's the Chevy. Find a place to park a block or so away."

Gabe parked the DeSoto in the shadows of some oaks. Irritation buzzed his brain. "This punk greaser's breaking into one of my rooms? One of *my* rooms." He glanced at Gabe. "A *fream* is somebody who doesn't fit in." He returned his focus to the Chevy. "Are we going to pound this asshole?"

"Pound?"

"Sorry. Are we going to beat the young man? Thrash the varlet within an inch of his life?" He jammed his eyelids closed until pain snaked across his forehead. *Why am I so mad?* Gabe took a deep breath of clarity. He mixed his words with the air as he exhaled. "I'm not hiding. This is my hometown, where I was born. Where do you live, Charlie Harris? You wear boots like I've never seen before. You don't seem to know much about what's going on in the world. If anybody's hiding, it's you."

"The boots are specially made. In between the layers of sole is an eighth-inch piece of steel. I'm a lumberjack. I cut down trees to make telephone poles. Too many of the men were stepping on jagged branch stubs and jamming them through their boots into their feet. The company came up with the steel plate idea, and there's a lot less injuries now. And I never said I wasn't hiding. I know I am. But if you really don't believe you are, you're an idiot, and I don't take you for an idiot."

Charlie touched his arm. Gabe jerked back.

"Sorry. Didn't mean to startle you. I just noticed you're wearing jeans, combat boots, and an army jacket. You were in the service?"

"Korea." Buried memories crawled out of the graveyard in his mind. He kept his eyes focused on the Chevy, away from the visions. "I didn't see any combat, though, just a lot of men who did. Alive and dead. I had to talk to them all."

"What do you mean?"

"I was the admissions clerk for a mobile evacuation hospital. Wherever fighting was taking place, we packed up and moved to be as close to the wounded"—he swiped at the tears—"and dead as possible. I was the guy who had to positively identify what was left of men who weren't men anymore, just pieces of meat." He clenched his jaw, gritted his teeth, and tried to will the visions back to their graves. Some retreated. Some didn't.

Gabe grabbed the steering wheel and wrenched it in his hands. His face was coated in tears and sweat. "My country would let me do that. My country's willing to let me try and live with those nightmares. But my country says I can't love who I want. I can't live the way I want." He turned to Charlie. He closed his eyes against the pain. Opened and closed them again. "What the hell did we fight to protect, Charlie? Just what kind of freedom did those men die for?"

Charlie pulled him close, stroked his hair. "I don't know. I don't know, Gabe."

Gabe pushed in, placed an arm over Charlie's shoulder and around his neck. For the first time since coming home, he felt... safe. His heart pounded in his chest. He rubbed his cheeks dry on Charlie's shirt. A tidal wave of desire swept over his body. Short snaps of breath pulsed in and out of him. His fingers dared to find the nape of Charlie's neck, the taut, leathery skin. He slid his hand upward, into the dense hair.

"Gabe," Charlie whispered.

He craned his neck, searching out Charlie's lips. Gabe pulled Charlie's head to his, parted his lips as Charlie's warm breath feathered against his skin. His stomach folded on itself. He tightened the muscles to quell the tremors of fear.

"Gabe. Johnny just got in his car."

"Shit." Gabe snapped upright. The wash of heat over his face changed from desire to embarrassment. "I got it, I got it." He fumbled at the key. Johnny whipped a U-turn and shot past them up the hill to the bluffs. The key turned, the engine started. Gabe slapped the shift into gear and sped after the Chevy, already lost in the darkness.

"Crap," Charlie huffed. "We can't find out who he's meeting if we lose him."

Gabe's eyes widened. "You think he's going to meet somebody?" *Compose. Compose, Gabriel. He just said that.* But the kiss of breath had awakened longing he hadn't known had gone to sleep. He wanted Charlie Harris. *Talk about rotten timing.* He beat away the thought with his eyelids.

"Yeah. Old Johnny boy wouldn't know what to look for on his own. Now he has to report he didn't find it."

Gabe grinned. Maybe he could actually help Charlie with this. And the knowledge felt good. "I think I might know where's he's going." He pushed the gas pedal down to keep the motor chugging up the steep hill to the bluffs. Wheeling the car around a turn, the incline doubled. Gravity pulled him back in the seat.

"What the hell? This is almost straight up."

"Hospital hill. The hospital sits on top of the highest point of the bluffs."

Charlie angled a look toward him. "He's going to the hospital?"

"The water tower's across the road from it. If the police chief sent him to your room, that's where they'll meet." The car rounded a curve and onto the crest of the bluff. Gabe pulled into the hospital parking lot and turned off the engine.

He pointed to a dirt road at a break in the trees. "That service road goes to the water tower. Last I knew this was still the only way in and out. We can wait right here and see who shows up."

"Last you knew?" A chuckle rose out of Charlie. "You used to hang out up there in the dark, did you? Here I thought I was the only one getting laid behind a tree."

"It wasn't like that," Gabe groused, then paused. He smiled. "Okay. It was exactly like that." He leaned his back against the door. "Except the first time." His smile expanded. "The first time was a disaster. It was so bad it didn't happen. Does that still make it the first time?"

Charlie folded his arms over his chest and grinned. "I have to hear this. Spill the beans."

Gabe chuckled. "How'd you know?"

Charlie drew his head back. "Know what?"

"I was still in school. I'd met a boy at a basketball game in a town north of Whistle Pass. We met under the water tower one night." He held out his open palms. "You know, they don't exactly teach how two men should do it in health class. We were both virgins. How do you tell your mother you don't want to eat her pork and beans because you're going to get laid?"

Charlie cracked up. Laughter rolled out of him. "You didn't."

"Oh, yes, I did. I was on my hands and knees. He spread my cheeks, and just when the head of his hard-on hit me, I blasted a note that could have sent factory workers to lunch break."

Charlie gripped his sides. His lips quivered; even more laughter spilled.

"Gets better."

Charlie twisted around, snorted glee. "Oh, God. How?"

"We were in the backseat of his car with the windows up."

Charlie's head tossed back and forth. "Stop. You're killing me."

"You'd have sworn a skunk died in there."

A black Cadillac came around the curve and entered the lot. Gabe grabbed Charlie and pulled him to the seat as the headlights swept over them. "Get down! It's Perkins."

The Cadillac slowly cruised past. The purr of the motor grew louder. Wheels squeaked on the pavement.

"What's he doing?" Gabe whispered.

"Checking the lot, would be my guess. Doesn't want any witnesses to the meeting."

The car passed by them again. Charlie poked his head above the door trim. "He's heading up the service road."

Gabe sat up. "Now what?"

Charlie's gaze remained focused out the window. "We wait. Just like with Johnny, Perkins wouldn't know about me or the picture if somebody hadn't told him. When he comes out, we follow him and find out who he's getting his orders from. I'm gonna have a cigarette." He grabbed his coat and climbed out.

Keeping his eyes on the lane, Gabe leaned against the door but watched Charlie out of his peripheral vision. Charlie walked to the end of the parking lot, illuminated under three pole lights, and lit a match. A splash of yellow momentarily painted his face. Gabe shivered. The man was so gorgeous. He'd come so close to kissing him but didn't know if the kiss would have been welcomed, or returned. He chewed on his lip, then chuckled.

Here he was in a car obtained under false pretenses, spying on the town's police chief, over a picture he had no business knowing about. God only knew what the outcome of all of this would be. If worse came to worst, he might have to leave the town he was born in and never return. He crooked a smile. For Charlie, he'd do it all over again. The corner of his smile collapsed. *Why?* The question furrowed his brow. Why, indeed. A running shadow sat him upright.

The figure bounded across the road into the lot. Gabe turned to shout at Charlie, but the man was nowhere in sight. Gabe sank onto the seat with his head up enough to see who ran past.

Johnny Upton blew by, hands covering his face. A parking lot lamp's light flashed red. Gabe swallowed hard. The hands were covered in blood. Johnny stayed on course to the Emergency Room door and flung it open. Charlie appeared out of the shadows and jumped in the car. The Cadillac rolled out of the service road and turned on its headlights once it was traveling north on the hardtop street.

"Let's go." Charlie looked at Gabe. "If you still want to. Otherwise, you can wait here."

Gabe turned the key and started the engine. He slipped the car into gear. "In for a penny, in for a pound." He goosed the accelerator, and the DeSoto flew onto the roadway. "What do you think happened to Johnny?"

Charlie shrugged. "Failure comes with a price." He lowered his brow. "Ours might too. You still have time to change your mind."

Gabe rolled his shoulders to shed the tension. He responded to the question by giving the engine more gas.

"You've some guts, hotel manager."

Gabe beamed at the compliment. "You too, logger."

CHARLIE wasn't sure if he would have returned the kiss or not. He wouldn't have pushed Gabe off him, and that awareness didn't comfort him. He'd come here out of love for one man, and now a total stranger had set his heart banging against his chest when the heat of Gabe's mouth brushed his lips. *Eye on the prize, Charlie boy.* He rubbed the back of his neck and glanced at Gabe. Just what the prize might be was starting to confuse him.

The car slowed. Lights glowed in the distance on the left.

"What is it?"

"Perkins pulled into Chandler's Steak House. There's a road just beyond it if you want me to make the turn."

"Yeah. Do that." Charlie craned his neck as they drove past the lot. Perkins pulled up to the doors of the building, stopped, then drove to an empty space in the center of the lot. Gabe made the turn onto the other road. "Pull over." Charlie opened the door and got out. So did Gabe.

"You don't have to come."

Gabe turned up the collar of his jacket. "Yes, I do." A shoulder rose and lowered.

Charlie nodded. "I understand. You need an idea of what those men felt before they died."

Gabe's head lowered.

Charlie rounded the car and pulled Gabe to him. "It's okay. It is. When fear chokes off your ability to speak, that's when you'll know. It's what they did about it that separated them from the others around them. Some ran toward the enemy. Some ran away. Some died never knowing who they really were. Others just stood, too scared to do anything."

Gabe's mouth was at his ear. "Your scars are in the front."

"In all the commotion, I got confused and ran the wrong way." His groin woke to the feel of the man in his arms. He pushed away before he surrendered to the blood flowing to the wrong place. "Stay low and behind me." Crouched, he tied his boot, then hurried through the trees, Gabe at his heels.

At the edge of the lot, Charlie duck-walked from car to car until he found a gap through which he could see Perkins's Cadillac. The window down, Perkins's fingers drummed the side of the door. Light footsteps clopped toward them. Charlie dropped flat to the ground. Gabe's weight at his ankles alerted him Gabe had followed suit.

The door swung open, and Perkins pulled himself out of the car. The man stood taller and wider than Charlie recalled, but they hadn't really taken the time to introduce themselves on the hotel stairway. Six two, an easy 250 pounds. The snap-brim hat was the same.

A shapely woman in a beige dress and heels strode around the back of the car. Dark blonde hair bounced on her shoulders. She hadn't worn a coat to the meeting. Obviously, she had no intention of staying long. Perkins's arms went wide. The woman threw her arms around the police chief's neck. Perkins enveloped her in his large arms and rubbed a paw over her ass. The woman's head bypassed Perkins's open mouth.

Charlie muted his chuckle. *No good news, no kissee.*

Her hands went to his shoulders. She backed up a step. Perkins's arms went wide again, and his lips moved as fast as if he'd just been caught cheating. The woman wagged a finger, spun on a heel, and stomped back the way she'd come.

Charlie flexed a cheek. She was attractive. Might even be pretty once she got the scowl off her face.

Perkins got in the car and backed out of the space. Acrid smoke flooded the lot, tires burned off rubber, and the squeal of the spinning wheels splintered the stillness. The car fishtailed onto the roadway and raced into the night.

Charlie laughed and turned to Gabe. "Old Perkins didn't get what he expected to get. I'd say an empty hand is all he's going to bed with tonight." Charlie froze.

Gabe's face was white as a dove.

"What's wrong?"

Lips moved, but no sound came out. Gabe gulped a lump Charlie could see roll down his throat.

"Charlie." Gabe closed his eyes. When he opened them, they glistened under a glaze of fear. "That was Dora Black. The mayor's wife."

"Isn't that interesting." Charlie stood. He turned and took a few steps toward the steak house.

Gabe grabbed Charlie's coat sleeve and jerked him to a stop. "What are you doing? You can't go in there."

"Why not?" One way or another, he had to meet Dora Black. She not only had the man he'd once wanted, she also apparently gave the police chief marching orders in exchange for a little backseat bingo. *Busy girl.*

"You have to have money to go in there. I mean, it's where the rich people hang out."

"I'll just have a beer. I'm sure I have enough for a lousy beer." He turned, but Gabe pulled him around.

"Charlie. You don't get it. Not just anybody can go in there. It's members only."

Charlie mulled that over. "Whistle Pass has so many rich people this place can survive? It's not exactly on the main road, you know. Up here in the hills, surrounded by trees." He looked around. "Not even a sign." Something definitely wasn't right here. "What kind of place is this?"

"A dinner club. Fancy food, lots of expensive booze. Only the finest clientele. Crème de la crème. A lot of business types come out from Chicago for *private* weekend meetings."

Charlie scratched the growth on his cheek. "Private meetings, huh." Yeah. Private as in screw your secretary six ways to Sunday and then go home to the wife and kids. "So, where're the rooms?"

Gabe looked away, his hand dropping from Charlie's coat. His gaze returned to Charlie. "There's a footpath behind the restaurant that leads to private cabins." The man took a deep breath and let it out in a deeper sigh. "I used to work weekends here as a maitre d'." He looked away again.

Reaching out, Charlie gently turned Gabe's face to his. "You met somebody. Nothing to be ashamed of."

Those soft gray eyes welled. "What it turned into is. Charlie, I—"

Charlie silenced him with a finger to Gabe's mouth. Dear Lord, the man had soft lips. "Your business. Nobody else's. Okay?"

Gabe slipped his hand around Charlie's and clutched it to his chest. "But I want you to know. I want you to know everything about me."

"Then maybe we should discuss it someplace other than this parking lot where I'm about to go meet the woman married to the man I once thought I'd spend my life with. Not to mention she's probably the one who dispatched the police chief to try and kick my ass. I'd kind of like to find out if she's running the show, or if she's the little woman dutifully obeying her husband."

Gabe's eyes shifted from side to side. "Oh."

"Yeah. *Oh.*" Charlie reclaimed his hand. He slipped off his coat and handed it to Gabe. "Wait here. If this place is like you say, I'll be right back."

The fact he wanted to hear every word Gabe wanted to share with him left Charlie more than a bit uncomfortable. Not about Gabe, but about himself. He didn't want Gabe to open up to him and then both of them discover Charlie was simply on the rebound. Gabe deserved better. Charlie allowed a half grin. The guy stood to lose everything by helping him, yet here he was.

He grabbed the building's door handle. Better to keep Gabe at arm's length until Charlie knew for sure just where Gabe stood in his heart. He hesitated. *In my heart? Where the hell did that come from?* He threw open the door.

CHAPTER 10

A BURST of heat blew over him. He looked up. A ceiling vent to warm the entering guests. The alcove decked out in fake stone opened to a hall. A scowling man in white shirt and black bowtie stood at a wooden pulpit. Behind the man was another wall. The opening to the man's right no doubt led to the dining room and bar.

"Do you have a reservation, sir?" The voice, more snarl than welcoming, came as sharp as the man's glare.

"We both know I don't. Tell Dora Black that Charlie Harris wants to see her."

The man's eyes stayed trained on Charlie while a finger slid over a page in an open book. "We have no guest here by that name."

A whiff of barbequed ribs and pork floated past. Charlie flared his nostrils. The food smelled damn good. Sounds of low voices and tableware on plates followed the food odors.

"Sure you do. You can tell her, or I'll tell her. Your choice." He deliberately rolled up the sleeves of his flannel shirt.

The greeter nervously tapped a finger on the page. Eyes darted right. "Let me check." The man walked through the opening.

"You do that." Charlie chuckled. Greeters in places like this doubled as security dogs on a leash. Without a visible master to turn this one loose, the dog had no bite. Charlie waited two seconds and then followed.

The bar was separated from the dining room by stacked beams forming a half wall. Rows of liquor bottles festooned the wall behind the counter and bartender. The stools and tables were filled with suited men and women in expensive-looking dresses. A few of the women even appeared close to their escorts' ages.

Charlie sucked in his cheeks. Not a one of these people would ever give somebody like Charlie the time of day, but they'd ask him for directions if they were lost. And, of course, he'd send them the wrong way.

The dining room was large and open. Round tables with seating for two to six. Linen tablecloths. Flowers in glass vases. Antlered deer heads littered dark paneled walls. A few diners looked up, flashed a distorted feature or two of disgust at Charlie, then went back to entertaining their table companions.

At a corner table for six sat the woman he'd seen in the lot. The greeter stopped there. She looked around the white-shirted man to Charlie.

A shiver traveled Charlie's spine. The woman's gaze scanned him like an X-ray machine.

Her left hand slid off the hand of the man seated next to her, who, in his late fifties to early sixties, clearly was not Roger Black. She lowered the stemmed glass of champagne she held in the other.

The greeter whirled. "Sir! You cannot be in here."

"It's alright, Ted." She stood, smoothing her dress as she rose from her chair. "I'll escort the gentleman out."

"Yes, ma'am." Ted wavered, narrowed his eyes and puffed out his chest, then he slinked past Charlie as instructed.

She came around the table and slipped her arm through Charlie's. A warm smile creased her lips as if greeting an old friend. "I'll just be a moment," she said to the three men and two remaining women. "Charlie knows my husband quite well."

Iceberg blue eyes shifted from cordial hostess to serpentine. Charlie gulped the realization he was a mouse in a snake cage. Gabe thought Police Chief Perkins was nobody to mess with. Perkins didn't hold a candle to this bitch. Unless the Roger of old had undergone a personality transplant, this broad had to have her puppeteer hand up Roger's ass.

"Don't you, Charlie?" She pulled him along beside her and whispered. "What do you think you're proving here? Are you trying to embarrass Roger? I won't let you hurt him."

Dora Black had crow's-feet at the corners of her eyes. She had a nice-enough-looking body under the dress, but the mid-forties Dora had about ten years on Roger.

"You marry Roger, or adopt him?"

Her mouth slithered into a wide smile as they walked. "A sense of humor." Her other hand brushed the hair on his forearm. Bile rose in his throat. "I like men with a sense of humor. You ever had a woman, Charlie?"

He tried to fight it back but failed—heat scorched his ears.

"No?" She pressed her cheek on his shoulder. "So I'd be your first?"

His free hand found the one on his arm and squeezed. Her head snapped off him. "That hurts." A crocodile smile crept back to her face. "You like pain, Charlie?"

They stopped at the door to the club.

The smile dropped like an anvil. "I can make sure you get all the pain you want."

It was Charlie's turn to smile. "Best send somebody better than the police chief. He didn't fare too well first time we met."

Dora released Charlie and took a step back. "Howard?" She snickered. "Chief Perkins is a dedicated civil servant." Her wink was cold as snake scales. "He seems to enjoy the servant role a little more than most."

A knot balled in Charlie's chest as a vision formed of Perkins, leather collar around his throat and attached dog chain held by Dora Black. *What the hell does Roger see in this woman?*

A plastic smile adorned her face. "I'm so glad we had a chance to finally meet. Roger's told me so much about you." She pushed open the door. "You'll have to come by the house for dinner sometime before you leave… permanently." She turned and walked away.

Unsure whether he'd screwed up with the ill-fated frontal assault, Charlie welcomed the chilly air. He inhaled and held his breath until his lungs ached. If nothing else, he'd found out Dora could be one hell of an enemy.

"You okay?"

He blew out the breath like smoke. Good idea. He pulled out the pack of Luckies and lit one. "Yeah. I'm fine. I need a bath, though."

Gabe chuckled. "She can make you feel that way, for sure. I damn near scrubbed all the skin off me the time she tried to fix me up with her husband."

Charlie bit down so hard he chomped off the end of the cigarette. "What? What'd you say?"

"Mrs. Black. I thought she was joking around at first. But she kept it up. Talking about what a cute couple we'd make. My shift ended, and I couldn't get out of there fast enough. The next weekend she introduced me to a business executive from Chicago." His face flushed and his eyes closed.

Charlie patted Gabe's shoulder. The hotel manager had more pain inside him than Charlie'd realized. And it made him want to hold Gabe and chase away the demons. "Don't worry about it. Last perfect man, we nailed to a cross. Let's get out of here."

They crossed through the trees to the car.

"Did you find out anything?"

Charlie shook his head. "Only that old Dora's a lot smarter than I am. She didn't tell me a thing." He ground out the butt and climbed in the DeSoto.

Gabe started the car and drove up the road toward town.

"You sure she wasn't joking about fixing you up with Roger?" Something beyond a pang of jealousy, just beyond his ability to identify, gnawed at him.

"I'm not sure anymore. It was a while ago. Maybe she was kidding."

"How long ago?"

"Right after the mayor got elected."

"How long they been married?"

"About a year before that."

He narrowed an eye. Maybe not so much a marriage for love as one of convenience and strategy. *Strategy.* Yeah. Something serious was happening in this town and had probably been in the works for quite a while.

Charlie looked at the shades of darkness passing by. He scratched at his beard. He really did need a bath. The thigh could use a good soaking too. "Look, Gabe. You've got a nice hotel and all, but there's only a tiny shower in the bathroom. I need a bathtub. Is there another hotel somewhere?"

"There's a bathtub in my apartment." The words tumbled out of his mouth. His hands twisted over the steering wheel.

Charlie flinched. "Oh shit." Naked in Gabe's apartment, while interesting, didn't sound like the best place to be right now. Not until he could figure out why the man made him think twice about the offer. The prospect of sex seemed good on the surface. But it was not knowing what was below Charlie's own surface that bothered him. He hadn't had time to figure out where Gabe stood within him yet.

"What? Did you say something?" Gabe slapped the steering wheel. "I promise to keep my eyes closed. Partially, anyway."

Charlie chuckled.

"There isn't anyplace else. You want a bath, it's my place or nothing. Of course, there's always the river. Little cold this time of year, though."

Thick rubber tires rumbled a memory of the newspaper's headline—*29 homosexuals committed to insane asylums.* Gabe was too nice a guy to play house with for a few days and then leave behind. And he would have to leave him behind. Gabe was safe from the world as long as he stayed in Whistle Pass... as long as he wasn't involved in the upcoming battle with Dora Black. A gentle letdown wouldn't work on a tender soul like Gabe's. The man would always be asking why they couldn't see each other and talk, or just be friends while hoping the relationship would grow. Every time they were together would be another huge risk for Gabe. Charlie sucked on his lower lip. This seedling needed to be cut before it took deeper root. And he only knew one way to do it. Charlie laid his head on the top of the seat and squeezed the words out of his throat.

"What's it like being a prostitute? You only bare your ass for the rich guys, or you troll us freams on slow nights? I'll bet you give a hell of a blowjob. Those extra? Or all part of the deal?"

The temperature fell through the floor. Gabe eased the car off the roadway. Tall grass scraped the undercarriage until the car stopped its momentum. With his foot on the brake, he popped the gear lever into neutral. His gaze stayed straight ahead, his voice distant as the Wisconsin pines Charlie wished he'd never left. The muffler's chug strummed the chords of silence.

Gabe's index fingers raised and lowered on the steering wheel. His gaze never shifted. "That...." His jaw worked back and forth. He dragged a hand over his face. "That really what you think of me?"

Charlie's guts rolled over and his temples throbbed, but he rotated his torso toward Gabe and held out open palms. "Who am I to fault a guy for making a little money on the side? So, what's the bath and bed gonna cost me? I don't have much cash."

"Please get out." The voice, empty of emotion, remained tightly controlled. "Please."

Charlie rubbed his palms on his thighs. "Suit yourself." He opened the door and climbed out. The car crawled onto the pavement and slowly, very slowly, gained speed until the taillights finally disappeared.

Charlie lit a cigarette and stared into the darkness. Cigarette between his fingers, he rubbed his forehead. Gabe was like all the others who'd never faced the wrong end of a gun. They all thought they wanted to know what they'd do when the bullets came at *them*, but truth be told, most couldn't handle knowing. They couldn't handle the fact they'd shit themselves, or cry, or be scared beyond a level of fear they never knew existed. Or that, no matter what they did, how they handled their fear, if it was their time to die... they'd die. And there wasn't a damn thing they could do about it.

Gabe needed to stay in Whistle Pass—where he was safe.

A wash of yellow light swept over Charlie. The car stopped a few yards behind him. A lasso of red light swung about him.

"You and me need to talk, boy."

Charlie tossed his coat to the ground. He placed his left hand over his right fist and cracked his knuckles. Then he exchanged one for the other and cracked the knuckles of his left fist. He turned and tried to see over the headlights, but the glare hid where the copper might be.

"Officer Austin." Charlie growled, clenched and unclenched his fists. "You have no idea how glad I am to see you. I hope you brought your sap, because I'm going to stick it up your ass."

Ka-chunk. Ka-chunk.

Every drop of blood in Charlie's veins plunged into his feet. Nothing else on earth made that sound—only a shotgun jacking a round into the chamber.

CHAPTER 11

GABE slammed the car door. Slammed the street door to his apartment building. Slammed the door to his apartment.

"Damn you, Charlie Harris!" He stomped over to the windows, spun around, and stomped his way to the bathroom door. He fixated on the grain of the wood—coarse, like Charlie Harris. And the door had once been a tree. Probably butchered by Charlie Harris and his little hatchet.

He drew back and smacked a fist into the offending symbol of his anger.

"*Ow!*" He shook his hand like Betty shook her dust rag. "Damn, that hurts."

He leaned a shoulder against the door and massaged his injured hand and bruised ego. A magnetic pull drew his gaze to the ceiling molding above the bed. Charlie Harris wanted to treat him like shit? Whatever game the lumberjack thought he was playing, Gabe had the power to end it right here and now and send Charlie Harris packing.

GABE parked the DeSoto alongside a sleek white Ford Thunderbird on the gravel lot. He glanced at the empty seat next to him and patted the photograph, tucked safely within his jacket's inside pocket.

"Screw you, Charlie." He opened the door and slid out.

He quickly scanned the other cars. A couple Buicks, a Lincoln, two Cadillacs, and a rusted green pickup truck. None of them were familiar, except the Thunderbird, and, of course, the pickup. The visible windows of the small, square red-shingle house had thick cloth shielding the activity inside. The front door opened. A giant of a man stepped out of the light and closed the door behind him.

"Private property. You need to go," said the pickup's owner.

"Lester, it's Gabe. I need to speak to the mayor."

The man's instant-oatmeal complexion brightened above the pitch cast around them by full pines on the sandy soil flats. Everybody in the area knew about the tiny house hidden in the tree grove in the middle of the watermelon, pumpkin, and potato fields. Rumors told of the monthly poker nights that ran until sunup. But they were just rumors, as no one around Whistle Pass had enough money to be invited to the high stakes games. No one except Roger Black.

"How ya doing, Gabe? What brings you out here?"

"I need to speak with the mayor, Lester."

"Why didn't you say so? I'll tell him you're here." The behemoth opened the door and disappeared inside.

"I did," Gabe grumbled.

Lester had been the biggest kid in school. Now he stood the biggest man in the whole county. Most said it was a shame his body outgrew his brain. But jailers didn't need smarts, and when Lester asked folks to cast their votes for the sheriff, folks cast their votes for the sheriff. Lester knew just about everybody in the county... and where they lived. You didn't want Lester stopping by a second time.

Mayor Black eased out of the house. He fastened the top button of his dress shirt and tightened the knot of his tie as he walked. Lester leaned out of the doorway and waved. "See ya later, Gabe. Say hi to Cathy, would ya? I got to go back to work."

"Why don't you tell her—" The door closed. Gabe lifted his chin in the air. "Yeah. Later."

Why Lester wouldn't speak to the restaurant waitress himself, God only knew. The whole county was aware Lester'd claimed Cathy as "his girl," and the poor woman hadn't been able to find a date in over a year.

The mayor planted a practiced smile on his face and strode to Gabe. He grabbed his hand and shook it fiercely. "How are you, Gabe? How's things at the hotel? I appreciate your putting my poster in the window. Need more campaign pamphlets for the desk? I can send some over."

Gabe retrieved his hand from the politician's clutches and stuck it in his pocket. The photograph weighed heavy against his chest.

"I wanted to give—" His eyelids snapped closed. He strained to reopen them. "I have something—" *Damn it! Just give it to him.* His heart pummeled his sternum. His brain pressed against his skull. Sweat soaked his armpits. He reached in his jacket and squeezed the picture between his fingers. Something out of place tickled the back of his mind. He glanced to his left, then refocused on the mayor.

Black's face turned to stone. His voice was ground gravel. "What do you have for me?"

The license plate on the Lincoln Continental was white with green numbers. The other cars all had the Illinois dark-blue background and orange numbers. Wisconsin plates were white and green. Charlie'd been working in Wisconsin.

Probably just coincidence. The muscles in his ass tightened. His feet numbed. *But what if it isn't?*

He left the photograph in the pocket and slid his empty hand out of his coat.

"I...." Gabe's mind spun like a Bingo ball cage. He needed to pick a reason why he'd interrupted the mayor. *Under the "I"....* "I wanted to let you know a guest asked about you." In his pocket, he scratched at his thumbnail. Of all the excuses in the cage, that ball seemed the least likely to roll, considering the mayor knew all about Charlie's arrival.

Black's jaw tensed. Through clenched teeth, he snarled, "Charlie." The candidate adjusted his tie, and apparently his self-control. A baby-kissing smile graced his features.

"Charlie Harris is an old friend. We served in the army together." He grasped Gabe's elbow and gently encouraged him toward the DeSoto. "He's not only a good man"—he stopped at the car and looked

Gabe dead in the eyes—"he's one of the few men I'd trust with my life."

The mayor opened the door. "You could do a lot worse than Charlie." He turned and walked away.

Gabe's face could have toasted marshmallows. He sat in the car and twisted the rearview mirror to see himself.

"Did he just tell you to date Charlie Harris?"

The face in the mirror simmered as red as second-degree sunburn. He closed his eyes and tapped his upper lip.

Oh, Gabriel, what are you doing?

He started the car.

"I don't know what I'm doing. Okay?"

The face in the glass scowled at him. Gabe scowled back.

"Here," he snarled. He jammed his fingers into his hair, kneaded it, twisted it, gnarled it. "Take that!"

He thrust his head back on the seat. "Asshole!"

Now he just needed to find Charlie Harris and figure out which one of them was the asshole.

OUTSIDE Charlie's room, Gabe rubbed his temples.

Johnny Upton hadn't bothered to latch the door when he abandoned his mission. The term "bottled hurricane" came to mind. There must have been an old crime drama Saturday matinee where somebody carved up a mattress and tossed stuffing around, and now penny ante thieves considered it a requirement. Did this idiot really believe Charlie would have disassembled the mattress and then somehow resewn it with machined precision?

Apparently.

Gabe kicked aside a wad of off-white fluff and entered.

"Damn." Six sheered sheep wouldn't have left as big a mess. The bedding lay in a heap. For whatever reason, clothing had been shredded and tossed like ticker tape. Charlie's duffle was in tatters. Gabe bent and picked up an orphaned handle.

"This kid's insane." He tilted his head to his shoulder. Dresser drawers had been pulled out and shattered. "Ohh. Now what did they ever do to you?"

The butterfly lampshade sat squashed atop a stomped alarm clock. Ironically, the lamp still stood on the dresser top.

A tan feather floated past his nose.

In a corner rested a pile of what had been pillows. A glint of brass caught his attention. He walked over to the mound of down and picked up a doorknob set. Two keys strung on a thin wire remained attached to the shaft. Against a baseboard lay a screwdriver.

He examined the door. Not a nick or scratch. Charlie was right; everybody in town must have a key. He gnawed on his cheek. *I'd have changed the locks too.* So, he did.

Cleaning the room was too large a task for this night, so he trudged down the stairs to the lobby. A man in a snap-brim hat sat on a couch, puffing on a cigar.

Fear eroded Gabe's stomach lining. He clenched his hands, put them to his mouth, and rubbed the bottom of his nose.

Police Chief Perkins rolled the cigar between his thumb and forefinger. A cloud of smoke rose to the fan above him, curled, then drifted downward.

"Kind of late for you to be out, isn't it, Gabe?"

Gabe looked to the counter. The weekend night clerk wasn't at her post.

"I told Grace to go get something to eat. Told her it'd be okay with you." Perkins slid forward. The leather upholstery squeaked as he stood.

Gabe tried to tell him it wasn't okay with him, but his throat collapsed onto the words.

Perkins pulled something from his pocket and slipped his hand into it. The cop twisted his wrist back and forth, ensuring Gabe had a clear view of what was to come. Brass knuckles. Gabe's heart beat its way to his brain.

Charlie's words clanged in his ears. *When fear chokes off your ability to speak, that's when you'll know. It's what they did about it that separated them from the others around them.*

Whatever happened, he had to protect the photograph. He took off his jacket containing the picture and hung it on the coat tree. He willed his sandbag-heavy feet to move. The best he could manage was a shuffle.

Perkins strode toward him. Light reflected off the metal on the back of Perkins's hand. Gabe gagged on saliva. Still, he put as much distance as he could muster between him and the picture.

Perkins's hand went low, back behind his waist.

Gabe swung his legs forward another step.

Perkins's sour body odor hit Gabe first. The fist landed right behind the nostril-closing smell. Gabe tightened his gut, but the blow crumpled him, drove through him to what felt like his spine. A hand grenade of pain exploded inside him. His lungs compressed and emptied. He smacked the hardwood floor face-first. He sucked at the air, tried trying to inhale. But nothing worked. He'd lost control. A stream of warm liquid coated his groin. Tears rushed down his cheeks.

Raspy breath sanded his ear. "Charlie Harris. He's got something I want. You're going to help me get it. I'll be in touch."

Gabe swiveled his gaze, saw the glint of metal coming at his head. Darkness swallowed him whole.

CHAPTER 12

SECONDS ticked their way into the past.

If Officer Austin wanted him dead, he'd have pulled the shotgun's trigger by now.

Charlie's expectation of dying on the side of the road ebbed slightly. He had to do something, though. Running wasn't an option. Nor was a suicide charge. Smartass seemed the next best choice.

"You want anything in particular? Or did you just want to hold something long and hard in your hands for a change?"

"I said we need to talk, boy. You got all bristled up like some stray dog. I wouldn't mind knocking your damned head off, but it'll have to be later. Get in the car."

"Why?" To get back to town, all Charlie had to do was stay on this road. Austin taking him anywhere else probably wasn't such a good idea.

"You're pretty stupid, aren't you."

A growl rumbled out of Charlie. Shotgun or not, he wanted a piece of Phil Austin.

"Dora Black and her friends will be along anytime now. Get in the damn car."

Hadn't considered that. Charlie slowly moved out of the headlights' beams to the passenger door. Austin climbed in. The cop leaned across the seat and opened the door. Charlie sat. Austin dropped the shotgun onto the backseat, turned off the rotating red light, and then sped down the road.

Charlie angled his body against the door and gave Austin the once-over. Near forty. Not too tall. Five eight, maybe. Grayed temples. Eyes a little too small for the round face. A slight second chin. Barrel chest and belly as big as a barrel pushed against the leather jacket. The man had some meat hooks—he could probably grab a basketball with one hand. Two knuckles on his right paw were enlarged. Charlie took him for a brawler; unskilled, but mean enough to counterbalance the lack of training.

"Where we going?"

The car slowed and pulled into the lane to the water tower.

Shaking his head, Charlie muttered, "You folks don't have much imagination."

Austin cruised past Upton's empty Chevy. The squad car stopped next to the rusty, skeletal support. Austin turned off the headlights, but not the engine. He tossed his cop cap onto the dashboard. His hand fondled the wood grips of the pistol in the worn leather holster strapped around his waist.

Charlie's hand went to the door handle.

"Relax." Austin's hand went from the pistol to the steering wheel. "It's a habit."

"Try chewing gum."

The cop's body jerked once. The corner of his mouth rose. Apparently the man had laughed.

"The mayor said you're his friend. Said I needed to apologize." The head moved about an inch toward Charlie. "Sorry." The ball of flesh shifted frontward. "Somebody's been threatening the mayor. Can't be too careful."

Fingers drummed the steering wheel. When they stopped, the man took a deep breath. "Why'd you let me do it?"

Fair question, so Charlie answered. "You were in uniform. If you'd wanted to really hurt me, you'd have unloaded that sap on me when I was trapped in the bathroom with you between me and the door." He left out the part about being out of control of his body at the time.

"Think you can take me?"

Charlie drew his head back. The man didn't mince words. "In a fair fight, yeah."

"I don't fight fair. Never have. Wanted you to know that, just in case."

A vein throbbed in Charlie's neck. Austin wasn't a likeable guy, but he had to respect the man's willingness to be upfront. No time like the present to see how far that willingness extended. "Where do you and Perkins stand?"

"Perkins works for Mrs. Black. I work for the mayor."

Charlie squinted in thought. Roger *hadn't* sent the telegram. Dora had. But how'd she know? He scratched at the hair on his face. Bliss hadn't accompanied wedded in the Black household. And in whatever war they had going on, missus got herself the police chief. The mayor didn't run his own police department. Which brought him back to Austin. "What do you stand to gain out of all this?"

"Perkins's job."

"Wouldn't it be easier just to screw the bitch?"

The cop's visible beady eye narrowed. Charlie snickered. "You tried, didn't you? Old Dora wouldn't have any of you. What's wrong? Needle dick?"

Austin's hand dropped to the pistol grip. "We're done. Get out."

Charlie had no sooner planted his feet on the ground than the car spun dirt and roared out to the street.

He lit a cigarette and looked up through the trees to the open heavens. The treetops swayed slightly in a breeze. Staying focused on the tree-touched sky, he stretched and rolled his shoulders, then let out a breath in a long sigh of loneliness. A pang rippled from heart to gut. He missed the forest and the night's stillness, broken only by owls' hoots. The air back home at the logging camp was clean and scented by pines and flowing streams. This air was awash in the stench of burning coal, exhaust, and the mixed assortment of diesel, fish, and other odd odors coming up from the river. He leaned a hip against Upton's car, closed his eyes, and wondered if Gabe could appreciate nights in the woods.

"Get the hell away from my car!" *Click.*

Charlie opened his eyes and smiled. "Thank you, God."

A hand grabbed his coat and spun him around. Charlie buried a fist into the bandaged face. The white gauze bled crimson.

Upton screamed, slapped hands over his face, and bolted back toward the hospital. Charlie picked up the abandoned switchblade and walked to the car. The rubber tire offered little resistance to the blade. He pulled back the knife. Air hissed out of the wound.

"Eh. What the hell." Charlie slashed the other three tires. He left the knife plunged into the driver's seat and casually strode to the road. Turning to begin the descent into downtown, he stuck his hands in his pockets, but a thought as solid as a brick wall stopped his stride.

Dora Black didn't strike him as an ignorant woman. Not at all. She wouldn't leave a potential tool like Phil Austin for Roger to use to his advantage. Unless Austin was actually a piece of yarn dangled in front of her husband for him to play with—while she held the ball.

Austin wanted to be chief. To do so meant Perkins had to be out of a job. If Roger got elected state rep, the mayor's chair would sit empty. Charlie pinched his lips around the cigarette and nodded. Perkins wasn't just in this for the sex; he was the next mayor of Whistle Pass.

Dora stood to own a state rep, a mayor, and a police chief without need of Charlie Harris. So why was he here? Charlie sucked in a drag off the smoke. He exhaled through his nose. The two streams merged into a pool and billowed into the night. Obviously, there was something at stake worth sacrificing Roger for.

Regardless of what that something might be, for now, he needed to talk to Roger and let him know he had a spy in his midst.

IN THE doorway of the hotel, Charlie massaged his calves. The walk down hospital hill, leaned back over his ankles and calves, had taken a toll. Hopefully the roach Johnny Upton hadn't torn up the room too badly and he still had a place to sleep. He grabbed the door handle. His throat cracked like dried paint.

Gabe was on the floor.

He flung the door open and ran. Dropping to his knees, he slid to Gabe's side.

"Gabe! Gabe." He stroked the cold cheek. He restrained himself from touching the swollen knot above Gabe's left eye. The right eyelid flickered. Ever so slowly Gabe's eye came into view.

"Pi...." He licked his lips and swallowed. "Picture. Coat pocket."

Charlie sat and tugged Gabe's torso into his lap. He held Gabe's head in the crook of his arm. "We'll get it. Don't worry about the picture right now. What happened?"

"Perkins." Gabe's tongue swept over his lips again. "He was waiting for me."

The beast in Charlie that always ran toward trouble roused. *Perkins. You're a dead man.* "Think you can get up?"

"Ye—yes." He drew in his knees. His face contorted in pain. His hands crossed on his belly.

Charlie pulled up the shirt. Four semicircles of red tattooed the skin. *Brass knuckles.* Perkins was going to be in a world of pain before he died. "You'll live. Come on, we've got to get you out of here." He scooted to his feet and lifted Gabe with him. Gabe's hand shot to his forehead.

"Oh, shit, that hurts."

"Wait an hour. You'll wish it only hurt like it does now."

"Picture." Gabe pointed to his jacket.

Charlie propped him against a couch. Gabe somewhat stable, he retrieved the army coat. He patted the material. The photo of him and Roger was in an inner pocket. He left it there and slipped the coat on Gabe.

"Couldn't think of a better place to hide it?"

Gabe's red-rimmed eyes watered. "Charlie, I—"

Charlie silenced him with two fingers against his lips. "Tell me later." He flopped Gabe's arm across his shoulders, steadied him with a hand on his ribcage, and headed for the hotel's exit.

Grace opened the door. "Boss? Are you alright?" Her mouth was open so wide Charlie could have scrawled "Kilroy was here" on her vocal cords.

Charlie coaxed Gabe forward.

As they passed the woman, Gabe muttered, "I have decided to retire for the evening, Grace."

AT GABE'S place, Charlie helped Gabe to the apartment's pristine bed. He almost hated wrinkling the smooth extra-large blue quilt. He sat Gabe on the bed's edge and pulled back the covers. His brain did a double take.

"You do know most men don't use lavender silk sheets, right?"

Gabe slipped off his jacket.

"I don't exactly host many pajama parties, Charlie, no matter what you might think." The words came out razor sharp and icicle crisp.

Knowing he deserved the sarcasm, Charlie winced and moved to stand in front of Gabe. "I didn't mean what I said. I just wanted to—"

Gabe's eyelids fluttered faster than hummingbird wings, then his eyes rolled back in his head. Charlie grabbed Gabe's shoulders before he fell and guided him backward onto the mattress. "To keep you safe," he said in a whisper to the unconscious man. He lifted the limp legs and turned Gabe so his body was completely on the bed. Tracing a fingertip over the wounded forehead, he focused on the budding knot of skin. "Apparently the *safe* part needs a little more work."

After untying the combat boots, Charlie gently tugged them off Gabe's feet and set them on the floor. Dignity required Charlie remove Gabe's soiled pants, so he did, with a quick tug and barely a glance at the plentiful bulge in the man's boxers. He pulled the covers over Gabe, then went to the bathroom where he soaked a towel in cold water. Back at bedside, he gently laid the cold compress over the goose egg. The jacket containing the photograph still rested on the bed.

"You've got some guts, hotel manager." Charlie leaned over and pressed his lips on Gabe's. They were heated and dry but tasted of sweet seduction. Charlie blinked and straightened. *What are you doing?*

He filled his lungs and eased out the breath... and the question. Not everything required debate or thought. Sometimes, the heart didn't need to know the why of it, just the who. A chuckle caught in his throat. The man's sculpted hair was a tangled mess. With his fingers, he caressed each strand into its proper place.

Charlie took off his coat and settled on the couch under the windows in the one-room apartment. He laid the pea coat over him like a blanket and stared at Gabe. The compress would need to be changed every half hour or so throughout the night to quell the swelling. He adjusted his shoulders under the wool coat and smiled.

His body hadn't so much as quivered after the confrontations with Austin and Upton. But those meetings didn't even register at skirmish level. Still, he couldn't deny the calmness within him where there should have been a gnawing need to crawl up and escape fear. Only one thing in his life had really changed—Gabe.

"Isn't this some shit," Charlie grumbled. "I don't even know his last name."

CHAPTER 13

GABE opened his eyes. Something was on his forehead. He pulled the damp towel off. Looking around the room, he quickly deduced he was alone and inhaled deeply. Charlie's fresh forest and tobacco musk crept up his nostrils. Wherever the man had gone, he hadn't left very long ago.

He rolled off the bed to his feet. The room's whirl and wobble sat him down again. Like a cat seeking a place to nap, pain kneaded, then sprawled across his belly.

"Okay." He gingerly touched the knot on his skull. "Let's take it a little slower this time, Gabriel."

Gabe focused on the bathroom and tub. A nice hot bath could definitely serve as the day's appetizer.

While the claw-foot tub filled, he undressed. The face in the mirror didn't resemble anyone he knew. The stranger was battered and bruised, but he sure did have nice hair. He smoothed the pillow-manufactured rumples with his open palm and smiled. Charlie had to have combed the mess the coiffure had been. The man's hands had been on him. Maybe his fingers had even run through his hair. Gabe's balls tightened. The dangling branch between his legs thickened to a limp log.

The reflection's gray eyes glistened with attitude. *Attitude*. Gabe stuck out his chin, slowly turning his head back and forth while focusing on his features. A satisfied smirk narrowed his lips. He'd stood his ground against Perkins. Granted, he'd gotten the shit beat out of him, but he hadn't run, or worse, fainted. The lump wasn't an injury—it was a badge of honor.

He glanced down at the web of red on his stomach. "Now this," he proclaimed, "hurts like hell." A grimace twisted his face. Rubbing the wound, he stepped into the tub and sank down into the cloaking warmth. The bar of Ivory floated past, and he stabbed at it with a finger. "Boom. Boom." The bar ducked under the water only to resurface. "Boom. Take *that*, Perkins."

Gabe rested his head on the porcelain and let the water's temperature seep into his bones. Charlie Harris had to have stayed the night, placing wet towels on his forehead. And, he'd combed his hair. He inhaled the rising ribbons of heat. If Charlie really thought Gabe was nothing but a whore, he wouldn't have done those things. *Would he?*

"No, he wouldn't have." He slapped the bar of soap. Water splashed his face and out of the tub. "Hee hee." Pleased with his conclusion, he bludgeoned the floating bar again. He licked his lips and… froze.

He ran his tongue over his lips again. A hint of tobacco danced on the tip of his taste buds. Had Charlie kissed him? *Wish I'd been awake for that!*

Gabe traced his lips with a finger. Charlie Harris cared. Gabe's heart thumped like the leg of a rabbit in heat. He grabbed the Ivory, scrubbed it over a washcloth, and whistled "Zip-a-Dee-Doo-Dah."

He had no idea what would happen once Charlie finished doing whatever the hell it was Charlie was doing. But for right now, Gabe had found a man who'd kissed him just because he wanted to, and if any opportunity, any opportunity at all presented itself, he was going to find out what Charlie Harris's lips tasted like, once he returned the picture to the safety of the molding above the bed.

THE restaurant rarely had many customers before eleven on Sundays, and today wasn't any different. Gabe plopped down in a chair at a table against the wall.

Pad and pencil in hand, Cathy strolled over. "Good morning, Gabe." Her jaw dropped a bit. "What happened to you?" She reached out and touched her fingertips to the painful mound. "Are you okay?" She furtively looked back to the counter. "We've got some aspirin. I can get you a tin."

"I'm fine, Cathy. Really." He smiled. Yeah. Life was good.

A brow rose in obvious doubt. Her voice discarded the friendly waitress tone. "What happened?"

"I tripped over a curb and hit my head on the sidewalk." *Okay. That sounded reasonable.*

She lightly touched the lump. "Well, be more careful, will you please?" Transferring the pencil to her free hand, she asked, "You want your usual?"

Tender muscles cramped in his belly. "Maybe just coffee this morning."

"Coffee and a small orange juice, coming up. You're hurt. You need the vitamins." She turned and walked to the counter.

"And a pack of Lucky Strikes," he called out after her. "And matches."

Cathy poured the coffee. "Why? You don't smoke."

"Thought I'd try once. Never know, I might like it."

At the blue and clear dispenser with a metal bar stirring the orange juice, Cathy filled a glass. "Whatever floats your boat, but I think you're making a mistake."

Cathy set the round Coca-Cola tray on the table while she placed the coffee, orange juice, cigarettes, and a glass of water in front of Gabe. She motioned to the water. "Just in case."

Gabe tore open the pack and tapped out a cigarette. He clenched it between his teeth like he'd seen Charlie do and struck a match. The match's flame heated the tip of his nose. He drew in a deep breath.

"Haawk! Gack!" His entire body lurched for the water. He grabbed the glass in both hands. His throat burned hotter than the match in his hand, which he dropped onto the table. The cigarette rolled until it nudged against the coffee cup. He gulped down every precious drop of water, then held up the empty glass. "More," squeaked out of his mouth.

He hacked bursts of smoke. His lungs tried to join the evacuation. He somehow managed to swallow them back into his chest.

Cathy held out another glass of lifesaving water. Gabe drank it without a breath, then set the empty glass on the table. He wiped the tears streaming down his face.

She sat in the chair across from him and took his trembling hand in hers. "This is because of the new guy in town, isn't it?"

Gabe pulled napkins from the metal holder and dabbed his mouth. He tried to pull his hand from her, but she gripped him tighter. The thought Cathy would think him a *queer* shivered his shoulders.

"Look at you. You're trying to smoke like him, you're dressed like him. Where's my friend Gabe? Is he still in there somewhere?"

Gabe fidgeted his feet in the combat boots. He scrubbed his face with a handful of dry napkins, then rubbed his chin on the top of the army jacket. She reached across the table and pulled his hand down.

"Don't you try and hide from me. We've known each other too long."

A thick sigh of surrender slid out his nose. But his throat clamped shut. He couldn't discuss this here... or ever.

Cathy massaged the back of his hand with her fingers. "Gabe." Her whispered voice was half scolding, half motherly. "We grew up on the same block. When my dad would come home drunk, Mom would send me to your house to spend the night. You think I don't know?"

She leaned over and kissed his hand. Jumbled, rubber band emotions balled and bounced around inside him as if his body was a pinball machine and the secret he'd thought to be well-hidden was the flipper.

"Shoot. Half this town knows, Gabe. The other half gossips."

He stared at her. *Shit. They all know?* He shot a glance to the door for an escape route.

Her grip tightened. "No, you don't. You're not running away from talking to me this time."

"Hey! How about some more coffee?" a gravel voice shouted from a stool at the counter.

Cathy put her chin to her shoulder. "Get it yourself! Can't you see I'm busy here?"

For the first time, Gabe noticed lines at the corners of Cathy's blue eyes, and a few more at the corners of her pink-lipsticked mouth. She wasn't but twenty-nine. Or was she thirty now? Ashamed he couldn't remember for certain, he closed his eyes to avoid her gaze.

No. Twenty-nine. She's only five years older than me. He met her gaze, eye for eye, and laced his fingers through hers. The skin was coarse, work-hardened. She'd put on a few pounds too. Her Marilyn Monroe body was leaning more toward Marilyn ate Judy Garland. He swallowed a lump of irritation. Why hadn't he seen before this how trying to raise her son right and working all the extra hours to make do had worn on her?

Gabe didn't have many *real* friends, and he'd ignored two of them long enough. He sat straight in the chair.

"I saw Lester last night. He said to tell you *hi*."

Her shoulders sank and she sat back, taking her hand with her. She crossed her arms and frowned. Bitterness dripped from her words. "Well, tell him to either tell me himself or shut the hell up." She sighed and shook her head. The nest of hairspray-coated blonde hair barely moved. "I'm sorry. I'm not upset with you." She rubbed her arms. "I just don't know why he won't talk to me, Gabe."

This was his chance to be the friend he hadn't been of late. "I think you scare him."

Her eyes bulged. "Me? The man's a monster. Boris Karloff would wet his pants if he ever met Lester. How could I possibly scare Lester Fricks?"

"Because he likes you, Cathy." Gabe sat back in the chair. "Did you know he's never been out on a date?"

She scoffed at him. "Not surprising. Who'd ever want a man so strong he changes flat tires without a jack, so bad-tempered nobody will ask me out on a date for fear he'll tear their head off, so dense he thinks Valentine's Day is a gangster movie—"

"And so kindhearted he taught your son how to play baseball."

Tears welled. She snatched some napkins from the holder and dabbed them away.

"Yeah," Gabe said. "I know all about that."

"Can I get some damn coffee!" the same voice from the counter snarled.

Cathy shoved out of the chair and stomped her way to the coffeemaker. Pot in hand, she leaned over the linoleum top and poured a healthy serving into his lap. The man bolted out of the restaurant, screaming all the way.

She held the metal pot aloft. "Anybody else want any before I finish my break?" The few remaining faces looked at anything but the coffee-wielding waitress. "No? Suit yourselves." She set down the pot and returned to Gabe's table, where she stood, hands on hips.

Gabe chuckled at her. "And you wonder why Lester's afraid of you?"

Cathy's face was etched with infuriation. "There's only two good men in this whole danged county. I'm looking at one of them. I can't get the other to even say 'boo' to me on Halloween." She stomped a foot and swiped at a renegade tear. "Damn it." Her lips tightened, and she drew a napkin over her eyes. "No one's ever done for my boy what Lester does. What do I have to do to get that man to talk to me?"

Gabe pushed out of his chair and stood. "What time do you get off?"

"Two. Why?"

"Can you have a meal ready by three?"

"Of course. You're always welcome for dinner anytime you want to come by."

"Not for me. I'd make plenty though. Lester's not a light eater." He headed for the door. Cathy caught him at the threshold.

Her hands trembled slightly and she clasped them together. "How can you—"

Gabe patted her jaw. "He'll be there." He pushed open the door but stopped when Cathy grabbed his arm.

She put her mouth to his ear. "This man you're interested in, if he's interested in you, it's not because you're trying to be him. Be you. I love you for who you are. So will he." Cathy planted a kiss on his cheek, then pushed him out the door. "Now, go forth and perform miracles."

HE FOUND Lester stacking engine blocks at the family business, Fricks' Salvage Yard.

"Why don't you use the chain hoist?"

Lester flexed a bicep bigger around than Gabe's thigh. "Good exercise." He strode over and shook Gabe's hand. "What brings you out here? Can I get you a soda pop or something?" A scowl draped the coarse face. Lester tapped a finger at his own brow. "What happened?"

"Accident. No big deal." Gabe shook his head. "What I want is for you to get yourself cleaned up. I'm taking you out for dinner. You up for that?"

A grease-streaked paw swept across the sweat-glistened butch haircut. "Sure. Getting hungry anyway. Where we going?"

Gabe couldn't completely hold back the grin. "Surprise. I'll pick you up at two forty-five. Okay?"

Lester shoved his hands deep into pockets in the sleeveless coveralls. The brow furrowed. "I don't like surprises." A smile broke through the indecision. "I trust you, though, so, okay. I'll be ready."

Gabe took a few steps and turned back around. "Dress nice."

A scowl dug into the pocked face. "Fancy, huh? You know I'm not a fancy pants, Gabe."

"Relax. Not that kind of place. But you can't be wearing blue jeans there, either. I'll see you in an hour."

LESTER stood waiting in the yard. Gabe, dressed in slacks and dress shirt to aid in the deception, snorted in amusement.

The man hadn't donned blue jeans, but the chocolate-brown uniform trousers with the beige stripe down the sides were apparently the only non-denim pants he owned. The white shirt was spotless. A necktie as limp as a dead snake dangled from his hand.

Lester opened the passenger door and climbed in. The DeSoto listed right.

"Needs springs."

Gabe put the car in gear and drove down the gravel road. "Now it does," he groused. He sniffed at the odor coming off Lester. The scent was thick and sweet. A yearning for pancakes awoke in Gabe's mouth. "What's that you're wearing? I never smelled any aftershave quite like it before. Reminds me of syrup."

"Smells good, don't it? I mushed up some blueberries."

Gabe groaned.

Lester held out the black tie. "I didn't know if I should wear this or not." His face flushed. "You'll have to help me if I do. I can't tie it."

"You know, the tie might not be a bad idea. Yeah. I'll help you before we go in."

Lester's nose rose. Nostrils flared. "What's that smell?"

"Flowers. Backseat." Gabe bit back the self-satisfied grin.

The massive head turned toward him. "What kind of place is this we have to bring our own flowers?"

"You'll see."

Ten minutes later he turned the car in to the trailer park entrance.

Lester oozed anger. He ground his palms into each other. "This is where Cathy and Richie live. What are you doing, Gabe?"

Gabe pulled over a few lots down from Cathy's. He turned off the engine and slipped the tie around his own neck to knot it. "You're having dinner with Cathy. She made a special meal for the three of you."

The man's eyes darted around the car like a spooked deer. "Three? Aren't you going to be there?"

Gabe cinched up the tie, then loosened it and slipped it over his head. "Put this on. No. This dinner's for Cathy, Richie, and you."

Lester tugged the tie over his head, had to lift it over the ear it caught on. Gabe tightened the knot, straightened the tie, and tucked it under the starched collar.

"You'll do fine. It's time you told Cathy how you feel, Lester."

The paws nervously rubbed the trousers. "What'll I say? I—I don't know if I can do this, Gabe. I mean, well, she's older than me, Gabe. She's got a kid and all. She's a lot more experienced than me that way. I've never been with a woman." He glanced at the floor. "One I didn't have to pay for, anyway."

Gabe leaned against the car door and didn't say a word. He knew the man well enough that he didn't need to speak, just look at him.

Lester gazed at the floor, the windows, the ceiling, the dashboard, and finally, at Gabe. A lip twitched, then a tight smile curled his lips.

"We were always the oddballs, weren't we, Gabe?"

Gabe folded his arms over his chest. "Yeah. You always came to my rescue when they made fun of me because I wouldn't take showers with the other boys in gym class."

Lester leaned back on the seat. Gabe hoped it wouldn't break under the strain.

The big man heaved a heavy sigh. "You were the only one who never called me 'dummy'."

Gabe briefly closed his eyes to allow the ensuing silence to renew their unique bond.

Leaning over the seat, he picked up the bouquet of roses. He handed them to Lester. "Mr. Carruthers unlocked the greenhouse so I could buy these."

Lester pushed his face into the roses and inhaled. "They smell good, like Cathy. Think she'll like them?"

"She'll like *you*."

Lester looked over to Gabe. Sweat beaded on his upper lip. "What am I going to say? I can't talk so good when I get nervous."

"Do you talk to Richie?"

The man's eyes lit up. "Oh, yeah. He's a great kid. Me and him talk all the time." A rush of excitement swept over him. Words flowed out in a single breath. "You should have seen him, Gabe. In the last game of the season, he hit a line drive up the middle that scored two runs. I was screaming from the stands I was so proud of him."

"And who was it taught Richie how to catch and hit a ball?"

Lester's eyes narrowed. A frown pulled down the corners of his mouth. "They were making fun of him. Nobody'd help him. Not his fault he doesn't have a daddy to teach him boy stuff." The brows lowered. "They had no business making fun of him, Gabe. He's only eight. He needed somebody to teach him is all."

"He needed a friend." Gabe reached over and patted Lester's hand as it strangled the long stems of the bouquet. "Kind of like us when we were growing up, huh?"

Lester calmed. "Yeah. Guess so. But we had each other."

"And now Richie has a friend too. He has you. That's what you talk to Cathy about. You tell her how proud you are of her son, how much joy he brings into your life. Trust me, the rest will take care of itself after that."

Lester's empty hand went to the door handle. "You're sure I can do this?"

Gabe kept his tone reassuring. "Yes. I'm positive. Get going before your dinner gets cold."

He swung the door open and put his feet on the ground. "I'm not a dummy."

The statement struck Gabe in the gut. "I never, ever, so much as thought you were, Lester. Why say that to me?"

Lester looked over his shoulder at Gabe. "Not talking about you. Mayor Black thinks I'm a dummy. The men he plays poker with do too. So I let them think that. They talk a lot, Gabe. Like I'm deaf or too stupid to understand English."

Adrenaline pulsed through Gabe's veins. "What did you hear you think I need to know?"

"They talked how you're a friend of some logging man that's in Whistle Pass, and how that man's going to take care of a problem for them."

Every cell in Gabe's brain shrieked. Had Charlie lied to him about not knowing why he was in town? If he had, what kind of game did he think he was he playing? "Lester, there was a Lincoln parked there with Wisconsin plates. Do you know whose that was?"

He shook his head. "'Thurston' is all the others called him by. I gathered he's some kind of big shot with the electric company. The mayor thanked him for his help in bringing the logging man to town."

Anger roiled in Gabe's gut. It added up. The electric company needed telephone poles. Charlie cut down trees to make the poles. Maybe the mayor hadn't known where to find Charlie, but the power company did. Charlie was in Whistle Pass because his former lover wanted him here. His anger turned to a growl. If they were, in fact, *former* lovers and weren't still seeing each other in secret.

But before he confronted Charlie with any of this, he needed to be sure of what he was talking about.

"Lester, is there a way to check and see if the electric company owns a logging firm in Wisconsin?"

"Sure. Even the power company has to register with the county in order to do business. The records should have most of their holdings listed. But the recorder's office won't be open until tomorrow."

"Can you meet me there? The clerk will probably help you quicker than he would me."

"Yeah, sure. Ten?"

"Sounds good. Thanks, Lester."

He held up the roses. "Thank you, Gabe." Worry painted his face again. "You sure I can do this?"

Gabe leaned over and massaged the man's tree-stump-thick neck. "Yes. Hurry up before Richie thinks you aren't coming."

"Richie?" Lester leapt to his feet out of the car and jogged down the street.

Gabe smiled contentedly at the success of his plan. Cathy had never even shared with Gabe the identity of Richie's father. While the town called her "slut" and whispers followed her anywhere she went the first few years, all that mattered to Gabe was that Cathy was his friend, and so he'd never asked. The woman had stood proud with her head held high against the gale of accusations.

Lester and Cathy. God help anybody who ever tried to come between them.

He leaned over to close the open door the big man had failed to close in his haste. The door jerked out of his grasp.

Police Chief Perkins plopped onto the seat.

The knot on Gabe's forehead throbbed. Fearful sweat flowed. In determination, he gritted his teeth. He would not run from this man—he clenched the steering wheel instead.

"Tomorrow night between nine and ten you be in the river park with Harris. I want you to kiss him. Don't screw this up if you don't want a court-ordered lobotomy." Perkins slammed the door behind him.

Gabe steadily breathed in and out in an attempt to control his fraying nerves. Perkins had just ordered a public display of homosexuality for which Gabe and Charlie could both be nailed to a cross. Gabe laid his head on the seat and blew out a ragged, terrified breath. The irony hadn't escaped his notice.

Judas had betrayed Christ with a kiss too.

CHAPTER 14

CHARLIE pushed the folding door of the phone booth closed and scrunched his nose. Somebody'd pissed in the thing. He yanked the door open. The phonebook wasn't any thicker than three comic books. He flipped through the pages until he found the right one, ran a finger down the list to *Black, Roger*, then lifted the receiver, dropped in a nickel, and dialed the number.

While he waited for someone to answer, he dragged his fingertips under the metal shelf. He struck a damp glob and jerked his hand away. Pink goo stuck to his skin. Bubblegum.

Scraping off the gum on the sharp edge of the shelf, he muttered, "What the hell's wrong with people in this town?"

"Hello? What did you say?"

Great. "It's Charlie, Roger. I need to talk to you." A man and woman in their Sunday best walked past. The lady's wide-brim blue hat fluttered with each step of her heels clopping on the sidewalk. "But not on the phone. Where can we meet?" The not-so-secret location across from the hospital immediately came to mind. "And don't say the water tower. Half this town does business up there."

"Really?"

Roger sounded surprised. Charlie rolled his eyes. "Yeah. Really. Where?"

"There's two taverns on Fourth Street just up from the Milwaukee Railroad's roundhouse. Meet me at the Nugget. The doorman will be expecting you. But I can't get there until after church, so, say, one o'clock?"

"Fine. See you there." He hung up and scratched at his beard. Captain Tom had said the bars on Fourth Street had slot machines. Not to mention it was Sunday and the bars shouldn't be open. Old Roger had definitely gotten into some stuff. He stroked the end of his nose. His gut tightened.

In the window of the closed dime store was a campaign poster with the state representative candidate's smiling face. Charlie gathered the saliva in his mouth and spat into a crack in the concrete at his feet. This Whistle Pass Roger Black was a man he didn't know... and sure as hell couldn't trust. A wrenching sadness gripped his heart. Not even a semblance of the man he'd loved existed anymore. He turned up his collar and stepped out of the booth.

If the Fourth Street bars were open, maybe Captain Tom's was too. He lit a cigarette and headed down the sidewalk.

The ship's wheel sign wasn't lit, nor were any of the beer advertisements hung in the windows. Charlie clicked the thumb-latch and pushed against the wood-framed door. Locked tight.

He cupped his hands around his eyes and peered inside. The glow of a light in some back room bled into the bar. All of the stools were upside down on the counter; the chairs were upside down on the tables. In the dim glow, faint shadows moved. Somebody was in there. He beat a fist on the doorframe.

Captain Tom's head poked into the light. "It's Sunday. We're closed."

"It's Charlie Harris! You set me up with a tab and an alibi if I ever need one."

The soft-bellied man strode into the room. Apparently the stained white shirt and suspenders were his trademark clothing. "Back already, huh?"

"Yeah. Quick turnaround."

Locks tumbled and clicked. The barkeep pulled open the door. He quickly looked up and down the street.

"Come on in. Got to be careful the cops don't see you." He closed and locked the door behind Charlie. "I can be in here on Sundays to clean and such, but can't have any customers. Unless, of course, we was on Fourth Street," he snarled.

Charlie followed Tom through pasty air laden with stale booze and nicotine. His boot soles stuck and smacked free of whatever had spilled and semi-dried on the floor. *So much for the cleaning excuse.*

In the center of the storeroom stacked with cases of beer and shelves of liquor, bags of pretzels and cartons of cigarettes, directly under a cage-covered shop light on an extension cord, stood a card table with four folding metal chairs around it. Tom sat on the empty one. The three other men ranged from the midtwenties to fiftyish. Smoke from a cigarette and one cigar in glass ashtrays spiraled to the ceiling. A man in a checkered flannel shirt shuffled a deck of cards. Dull snaps from the cards bounced off the walls. Another man in a black shirt with the top two buttons open fidgeted with a pencil over a scorecard. Open bottles of beer rested on the floor next to the feet of the men.

Tom pointed at each one during the introductions. "Terry, Tony, Ted." A chuckle clattered out of Tom's throat. "We call this our Sunday T party." He pointed with his chin to a man seated between two stacks of metal shelves. "That there's Edgar. He doesn't play euchre. Everybody, this here's Charlie Harris, a railroader staying at the hotel. Edgar, you might already know him." Congeniality drained from Tom's face as he focused on Edgar.

Charlie understood he was being checked out. His muscles tensed, and he clamped his teeth together in readiness for the night clerk to reveal Charlie wasn't any railroader. He clenched his hands into fists in his pockets, just in case he had to fight his way out of there.

Edgar merely nodded once, then took a sip of gold liquid in a glass and petted the sleeping dog on the lap of his bib overalls. But his gaze didn't leave Charlie.

Tom's stern voice said the man wasn't convinced. "Everything all right, Edgar?"

Edgar glanced at Tom and shrugged. "Yeah. Fine. He's a freelancer for the CB&Q." He looked back to Charlie. "The Burlington. Freelancers sometimes have to hang around for an extra day or two until a crew needs an extra hand." The man shifted his focus back to Tom. "So don't go getting your nuts in a vise if you see him around more than some of the other men." He took another sip and ignored Charlie.

Tom settled into the chair. "Deal the damn cards. I'm down forty cents."

Charlie's chest sank in relief as he uncurled his hands. Why Edgar lied was a mystery, but a grateful one.

"I order it up and I'll play it alone. Help yourself to a beer out of the fridge. Leave a quarter on top."

Charlie meandered over to the round-top refrigerator and pulled out a Busch. He snapped off the metal cap on an opener screwed into the wall. Setting the bottle on the floor, he pulled his rubber change holder from his pocket. A quarter hid under the pennies and dimes, and he dropped it into a glass half-filled with quarters. He returned to the game in progress and leaned against the wall.

"Ha! Ran 'em. Mark down four points, Terry." Tom shot a look to Charlie. "What brings you out this morning?"

Charlie watched Tom's partner rub his nose and fondle the top of the second card in his hand. The man to Tom's left, Tony, dug in his right ear with a fingertip. When Ted, Tony's partner, scratched his chin, Tony dug in his left ear. Charlie stifled a laugh. This cadre of friends was cheating. No doubt they knew each other's signals as well as they knew the back of each worn card, so the playing field was still even.

"Had some time to kill. Figured I'd get a beer."

Tom growled. "How'd we lose a point?"

Tony offered the answer. "You pulled the hair in your left nostril for spades when it should have been your right. You confused your partner. Jeez, Tom, get your signals down."

Tom grumbled and gulped a few swigs from his beer. He set the bottle aside while the next hand was dealt. "You staying away from the butt packer?"

Charlie tensed. His hand went to fist. He really didn't like Gabe being talked about that way. He noticed Edgar squint an eye at Tom, then take a long drink. Edgar closed his eyes.

The old man not only knows, he doesn't want to be a part of the talk.

"Yeah. I'm curious, though. What if I find somebody doing that queer stuff?" Charlie asked.

"You tell us." The gruff voice belonged to the fiftyish Tony. "We'll take care of it." He swiveled and stared at Edgar. "No matter who it is."

Edgar's glassy eyes snapped open and burned hot. "Gabe's okay. He never done nothing wrong while I was around. You leave him out of this conversation. You want to give somebody a knuckle sandwich, you find somebody else. I may be an old drunk, but me and Muffin can still kick your butt."

Tom turned peacemaker. "Edgar's right, boys. We don't talk about anybody local unless we have proof. Those are the house rules. But if we ever do"—he looked at Charlie—"we'll clean his clock and then some. You see a queer, you just let us know."

Terry chuckled. "Got that vat of tar over at the roofing company. I'll bet we could get some feathers from old pillows at the furniture store."

"Thought we were saving the tar for that colored family who moved in on Becker Street," Ted said.

Tom took charge. "I'll take coloreds over queers any day. Pretty easy to spot one when we want to play a little, even for a nearsighted fool like you. Pink undies are a bitch to see without getting in a queer's pants, though. 'Course, maybe you'd enjoy unzipping some flies for us, Ted."

Snorts and guffaws fell out of the card players. Edgar quietly petted the dog.

Charlie took a hit off the beer in his hand and studied the quartet over the bottle. Apparently, this was the heart of Whistle Pass' version of vigilantes. He wasn't quite sure what to do with this information yet, but something chipping at his brain hinted these morons could come in handy.

"If you've got another chair, I've got a couple hours to kill"—he tossed his red rubber change holder on the table—"and money to lose."

Tom slid his chair to the side. "By the fridge. You can slip in beside me. That way I won't have to reach so far for my winnings."

Charlie grabbed the back of the folding chair and snapped his wrist to fling it open. He slid the open seat across the floor to the table. Turning, he stuffed a dollar bill into the glass on top of the fridge. "You boys ready for another round? I'm buying."

"Hell yeah," came the unified response.

Charlie watched closely as the four men chugged down the remnants in the bottles. He pulled four beers and walked over to the table. Tom produced a church key and popped off the bottle caps, which clattered onto the floor one by one. Charlie sat and angled his seat to prevent the men at his sides from seeing his cards. They'd all exposed their signals while he'd patiently waited, and now he'd use their own signals against them. He also had another advantage. When these beers were half gone, he'd buy another round, and the men would chug the remnants of these just like they had the last ones.

Chugging beer numbed common sense.

He stole a glance at Edgar.

The old man leaned over and hugged the dog. A subtly raised thumb appeared from behind the Chihuahua's head.

Charlie gave a short, slight smile in return and focused on the cards being dealt.

Gabe had an ally in Edgar. And now, for whatever reason, Charlie did too. But would the unspoken alliance extend beyond the few paltry dollars he'd pilfer from the pockets of these backyard bigots?

He didn't know. That chipping at his brain said he might soon find out.

HE'D kept the fleecing to a minimum. Four bucks—two for the beers he bought, and two for supper later on. Tom and the boys invited him back any Sunday morning he was in town for a shot at winning their money back.

Edgar sipped his whiskey and offered no acknowledgement when Charlie left Captain Tom's. Unsure which way Edgar would lean when the chips were down, the old man remained an unknown in Charlie's mind.

He rounded the corner from Chicago Avenue onto Fourth Street.

On the next block, across the street, stood two old three-story brick buildings. One housed a café—closed. The other, a secondhand shop—also closed. On the corner ahead of him, a yellowish concrete building with a flat roof sat like a building block out of place. The side facing him was a blank wall. The few houses in the area were all two- and three-story with peaked roofs and lattice. A cement box just didn't fit in—more "get it up and screw the aesthetics" than anything else.

A solitary porcelain-on-metal Old Milwaukee sign dangled from a black iron support. Charlie guessed he'd found the Nugget.

He crossed the street to the next block littered with a dozen or so parked cars. Two windows too small to crawl through were nestled into the cement fronting about eight feet up from the sidewalk. A windowless gray steel door simply had "Nugget Club Members Only Knock for Entry" painted in gold lettering. He continued on to the next doorway in the structure. Same kind of gray steel door: "Archer's Place Come On In."

Charlie tried the door—locked. He shrugged. So much for the "Come on in" part.

He walked back to the Nugget and focused on the E in "Nugget." A peephole.

A diesel locomotive revved its whirring engines. Charlie leaned back and looked down the street. An orange and black Milwaukee Railroad engine eased out of the roundhouse where the street met the multitude of tracks. Black smoke heavy with unburned diesel billowed, sank, and sloshed around the slow-turning wheels. The stench flowed through the neighborhood.

Charlie swiped at his nose and gazed up at the sign above his head—Old Milwaukee. He smirked at the irony. Somebody had a sense of humor. He banged on the door with a fist.

Locks turned and the door opened.

"Well, well," Charlie said to Phil Austin. "I suppose this shouldn't come as a surprise."

"Mayor's expecting you." Austin, clad in black slacks, white dress shirt, and black pencil tie glowered and nodded toward a closed metal door at the back of the room off the end of the immense bar.

Charlie scuffed the soles of his boots across the coarse concrete. The floor had been poured without much concern for professionalism. The bar, as long as the wall, minus the door at the end, was constructed of painted plywood and pine. Mirrors reflecting the varied colors of the contents of liquor bottles hung behind the shelves, but the mirrors were all beer and whiskey advertisements, not built-ins. Three sets of long-stemmed tap handles poked up from the counter. Stools lined along the front had round wooden seats on chrome legs. The bartender, thirties probably, wore the same apparent uniform as Austin and stood chatting with the one visible customer. Metal-legged tables with linoleum tops and a variety of undoubtedly secondhand chairs haphazardly covered the floor. Each had a large glass ashtray in the middle. The walls had been painted gold with no decorations of any sort.

Charlie scrubbed the back of his teeth with his tongue and wondered if Roger owned the used furniture shop across the street too. Owning the place you bought your accoutrements from had to be a benefit, and a tax dodge of some sort.

What struck deep in his mind was how quiet the place was. No music, no sounds of slot machines, no... nothing, except for the idle mutterings of the two men talking to one another—until he gauged the width of the room. The quiet took a backseat to the fact quite a few feet seemed to be missing. He wanted to go back outside and take another look at the length of the building, but Austin walked around him and rapped on the door. It opened to a man in, again, black slacks, white shirt, and black pencil tie. The shirt strained against well-developed muscles.

Whirs of slots, clinks of pulled metal arms on the one-arm bandits, laughter, an occasional curse, a scrapbook of voices, and odors of cigars, cigarettes, and smoked meat climbed the narrow stairway to the right.

"Mayor wants to see him." Austin turned and strode away.

Charlie raised a brow. The scars on the man's face resembled gravel roads. This guy had been worked over more than once, and probably learned some hard, painful lessons from it—lessons he'd be only too willing to share with anybody he got turned loose on.

Roger had himself a junkyard dog of a bouncer.

The man stepped aside. Charlie took mental note that there were two doors, each with thick layers of Styrofoam attached to the back—sound buffers. The whole building had probably been decked out with sound insulators.

Which Charlie found interesting. The entire town seemed to know about the slots and gambling, but serious effort had been made to abort the actual physical awareness from inside the building.

On the other side of the landing, the man knocked on a door, then opened it. "Somebody Mr. Austin says you wanted to see."

Mr. Austin? Another interesting quirk.

The man gripped the doorknob and walked, pushing the door until it was fully open. Charlie entered the room and the door closed behind him. He checked. The man hadn't stayed.

The room's walls were covered in dark paneling. A Moroccan leather couch rested against a wall. Two matching armchairs sat across from it, a coffee table in between. Floor lamps in three corners provided diffused lighting. Roger swiveled back and forth in a black leather chair behind a wooden desk. A rug echoing the leather covered the floor. A hint of lemon permeated Charlie's nostrils.

"Nice digs."

Roger selected a pencil from a holder on the desktop and slid it from one hand to the other and back again.

"What did you want to talk to me about? Did you hear something about whoever's threatening me?" The stony look on the man's face didn't suggest he expected any news. He also didn't invite Charlie to have a seat.

Charlie spun one of the armchairs around on its leg and sat facing his former lover.

"I think you already know."

A smile sprang across Roger's face. "I heard you met Dora. She's quite a woman, isn't she?"

Inside, Charlie cringed. He'd blindly thrown out a dart and hit the target. *If* Roger was being threatened, the culprit was none other than Roger's own wife, and Roger knew it. So, once again, just what the hell was he doing here?

"What game are you playing, Roger? You don't need me here."

Roger stuck the pencil in the holder and leaned over his arms on the desk.

"Yes, I do, Charlie. I can't trust anybody anymore. I don't know what's going on. If it is Dora sending me death threats, I don't know why." A twisted smile contorted his features. "You've probably figured out I can't ask the police chief to look in to it." He pressed back in the chair and drummed his fingers on the arms. "It's like every time I do something, Dora already knows about it. She's always a half day ahead of me."

The question of why Roger's wife needed to be ahead of him slogged its way to the forefront of Charlie's mind. But first things first.

"Austin's working for your wife. Did you know that?"

The color in Roger's face went darker than the rug's maroon. He plunged a hand under the desk. The door *swooshed* open behind Charlie.

"Yes, sir?"

Roger has a hidden button to call his dog to heel. Roger really wasn't somebody he even wanted to know anymore. Still, Charlie filed the information away for future reference. And that confused Charlie as well. Why didn't he just go pack his bag and leave this town? He heaved a sigh. As much as he wanted to leave, some unexplainable weight had burrowed into his chest and wouldn't let him walk away.

Roger swatted a drop of spittle from his mouth. "Tell Austin to get his ass in here!"

"Yes, sir." The door rubbed over the rug.

Roger thrust an open palm into the air. "Wait a minute."

The sound of the door closing stopped.

He lowered the hand and tapped at the desktop. Finally, he narrowed his eyes. "Never mind. Forget about it."

The door clicked closed.

Okay. Now what's up? Charlie folded his hands, rubbed his chin over his index fingers, and waited to find out.

Roger ground his palms into his cheeks. "I'll use that son of a bitch just like Dora's been using him." He crossed his arms and stared at something beyond Charlie.

Charlie offered a suggestion. "Get rid of him. You have that animal outside the door."

A growled chuckle emanated out of Roger. "Austin did that to his face. Twice." A look of concern melted the anger. "Be careful around Austin, Charlie. You don't know how dangerous he can be."

Charlie did his best not to let his own anger show itself. *You're telling me this now?* "Thanks." He needed to get out of here and be rid of the mental stench of what Roger had become, so he stood to go. But he still had another question. "How would Dora know about me and the picture of us kissing?"

Roger looked at everything but Charlie.

The avoidance of eye contact hit him like a bus. "Shit. You lied to me when you said you never told anybody. You told her." *What the hell?*

Roger laid his hands flat on the desk. "It was years ago. How did I know she'd try and use it against me? Candlelight, wine… we were in love. We shared our innermost secrets with each other one night." He looked up at Charlie with puppy dog eyes. "I'm sorry, Charlie. I really am. More than you could know, but I need your help. Please?"

This whole situation was pissing him off. "Help with what? I'm getting tired of the games, Roger."

"Don't you see? She wants to destroy me."

Charlie bit back the rage boiling in his belly. But he knew it wouldn't be long before it spilled out, and he'd have to find a place for it to spill.

"Why? Why, Roger? Tell me. She stands to gain everything if you get elected. What the hell is going on?"

Roger slapped the desktop and jumped to his feet. His voice went up an octave. "I don't know! That's the whole problem. She acts like nothing's wrong, we play charades of the happy couple, and behind my back she's screwing my own police chief, and now, out of the blue, here you are. I. Don't. Know. I wish I did."

Charlie threw up his hands. Enough was enough. Dora and Roger deserved each other.

"I'm done with this. You and the little woman have a nice life, Roger." He turned to leave.

"Austin told me you've been seeing Gabe Kasper."

Charlie's feet froze to the rug. His ears and cheeks flamed.

"Yeah, Charlie. You just told me Austin's working for Dora. So, she has to know about it too."

Charlie's lungs emptied in a rush out his nose. "And if Dora knows, Perkins knows." That explained the real reason behind the attack on Gabe. Charlie had been sent a message, and he'd misread it, or rather, hadn't read it at all. He had to talk to Gabe and find out exactly what happened.

Christ! Why hadn't he become a cop instead of a logger? This whole mess would sure be a lot easier to understand and deal with if he had some training. Instead of just wanting to punch people's lights out, he obviously needed to actually talk to people. People like Gabe. A ball of heat coaxed some sweat from between his thighs.

The unidentified weight holding Charlie in Whistle Pass did have a face, and a name. *Kasper. Gabe's last name is Kasper.* His heart glowed the smile his face couldn't right now.

"They'll hurt him, Charlie. You know they will."

The smiling heart went deadly still and cold. Yeah, they would. And it would be all Charlie's fault for having Gabe play chauffeur. He slowly turned back to Roger with a stern plea of his own. "Gabe shouldn't be involved in whatever war you and your wife have going. Leave him out of it."

The overgrown rat scurried around the desk. Roger grabbed Charlie's shoulders and looked at him with the most sorrowful look it had ever been Charlie's displeasure to see. He wanted to puke.

"Give them what they want, Charlie. I'll deal with the consequences. Give them the picture. It's the only way to keep Gabe safe."

Charlie opened his mouth to say he would, but a glint flashed in the back of Roger's eyes and then vanished just as quickly, like a sparkler's single spark. Charlie didn't know what it was, but that damn creature inside him that kept him alive by running into danger, shivered. Something still wasn't right, and might be terribly wrong.

"I told you I got rid of that photo years ago."

Roger pulled Charlie tight against him in an embrace. Hands stroked Charlie's back. One went to the nape of his neck. Charlie restrained himself from belching his nausea in Roger's ear. But he did have to admit the man smelled good. The aroma reminded him of lemonade, thus the hint of lemon in the room. He focused on the aftershave and not the body he'd explored with his mouth and tongue in another lifetime.

A hand went to Charlie's ass and pushed him into Roger's groin. The pea coat served duty as a most welcome shield. Roger's lips found Charlie's neck, and a wet tongue flicked over his skin.

A memory of the two of them in a barn loft surfaced. The moon's rays splintered through bullet-riddled boards. The straw, though moldy, had smelled of paradise that night when Charlie surrendered to Roger's physical desires. He'd spread his legs and taken Roger inside him from the top to relish his lover's body on his.

Charlie tilted his head back and moaned.

A whisper of a time gone by played at his ear. "Need you."

Need you. They had been Roger's code words. *Need you.* He said them every time he wanted to make love to Charlie. *Need you.*

But they weren't in love anymore. And Gabe Kasper was a hell of a lot more man than Roger Black had ever dreamed of being.

Charlie shoved the memory halfway across the room.

Roger fell against the desk. The holder tipped and pencils rolled in angles. His eyes grew wide and round in shock. "What? Charlie? What?"

An acid taste of disgust filled Charlie's mouth. He spat it onto the rug, wheeled around, and headed for the door.

A quavering shout filled the room. "You're going to have to stop them, Charlie! One way or another. You better think about *that*. Is Gabe worth killing for, Charlie? Because it might be the only way to save him."

Charlie flung the door open. The obedient dog opened the next one.

He stormed his way out of the club into the diesel-laden air and drew in all the unpleasant smell he could to smother the remnants of Roger's odor. Charlie flopped his arms on top of his head and inhaled another lung-filling breath. A stench of ripe garbage dug at his nose and flared a nostril. He lowered his arms, and the stink wafted into nowhere. He raised his left arm and sniffed the pit of his coat.

Damn. It wasn't garbage—it was him.

Charlie stuffed his hands in his pockets and hustled along the sidewalk.

His eyes burned. It'd been a day or so since he'd had any real sleep. But before he laid his head down, a little soap and water to clean the funk off his skin wouldn't hurt a bit.

When he woke, he'd decide who needed to die to keep Gabe safe. Because Gabe Kasper *was* worth killing for… and then some.

CHAPTER 15

IT HADN'T been easy, or fun. Gabe surveyed his handiwork and nodded his approval. Room 412, Charlie's room, once again stood guest-ready. He opened the door. The miniscule breeze sent an errant feather skittering across the floor. Gabe snagged the culprit and jammed it into his jeans pocket. He closed and locked the door behind him.

Each footfall on the old wooden steps tolled his turmoil. But his harbinger of doom wasn't a gallows erected in the center of town. No. His would be a park bench by the river... and a kiss from lips he wanted to spend eternity glued to.

Self-loathing knotted a muscle in his chest. He rubbed the tightness as he descended the stairs. His other palm he lightly slid along the banister for support. Life was only necessary to live.

He snorted disdain. Life in Whistle Pass had been acceptable. Safe. Out in the big world, people like him—homosexuals—were scorned, imprisoned, had experimental surgery performed on their brains, beaten, and, he gulped, killed.

Now Charlie Harris threatened to destroy his sanctuary from life's realities.

The metronome of betrayal transferred from his heavy steps to the deep tick-tock of the lobby's grandfather clock. He paused on the bottom step. Two men sat on separate couches. One absently flipped pages of a magazine. The other read a newspaper. One wore jeans, the other bibs.

Railroaders. Men lucky enough to only be passing through—spending a few hours to rest before they climbed aboard another train and headed home to whatever lives waited for them.

Light glinted off metal on the magazine reader's left hand. A wedding ring. The man was married. Probably had a family to go home to. The knot in Gabe's chest wrenched even tighter. He dug fingernails into the discomfort. He'd never know what it was like to be married, legally committed to one person, let alone have children.

His thoughts wallowed through the mire of uncertainty to Lester and Cathy. That they'd marry held no doubt. They'd only needed a push toward the altar. Their lives would be happy, and they'd raise Richie to be a good, strong man. Gabe smirked. Hopefully a good, strong, *straight* man.

"Everything all right, Mr. Kasper?"

Gabe looked over to the desk clerk. "Yes. Fine," he said, knowing nothing was fine or all right. He strode to the check-in counter and set down a key.

"This is for 412. Please make the change on the room tag." He turned and stepped toward the exit. "Thank you."

He paused at the door and looked over his shoulder at the lobby with the couches, chairs, and slow turning fans, inhaled the aroma of years of guests, smoke, sweat, cleaning agents, Betty—his life. He clenched his jaw to fight back the pooling tears. Tomorrow might be the last time he'd ever see the cocoon of safety he existed in. If he followed Perkins's orders, he might have a chance, though. Maybe Perkins would let him walk away after he tricked Charlie. He closed his eyes. Maybe he wouldn't kill himself after he tricked Charlie. He slowly opened one eyelid. Could people still kill themselves after a lobotomy? A shiver descended his spine, vertebra by vertebra, then climbed back up to bury a dagger of pain at the base of his skull.

Gabe coughed and pushed open the door.

GABE sat on a stool in the restaurant. An "Ahem" drew his attention. He looked up. The waitress stood in front of him.

"I'm sorry. Did you say something?"

She held a pad and pencil in her hands. "I asked if you wanted the fried chicken. You know, the Sunday Special? You always order it."

Gabe moved the salt and pepper to equidistance from the napkin holder.

"No, thank you. Coffee is all."

"How about some cherry pie? You always have cherry pie on Sundays. I made sure to save you a slice. With a scoop of ice cream? On the house."

He ran his thumb over the metal top of the pillow-glass saltshaker.

"This is dented."

She snatched the shaker and exchanged it for another from the next condiment station on the countertop. "Better?"

He rubbed the top, felt no deformities, and adjusted the shaker to its proper place.

"Yes, thank you. No pie. Just coffee."

The waitress turned to the coffeemaker. Gabe glanced at the sorry excuse for a human being staring back at him from the mirror. What kind of man would even consider saving himself at the expense of a friend? He blinked twice. Charlie Harris wasn't a friend. His heart thumped against his chest, the knot wrenched even more pain from him. Charlie Harris was a man he was falling in love with. Gabe scowled at his reflection. Not "falling." He loved Charlie Harris.

A din of muffled voices assaulted his ears. He looked beyond himself in the glass. There were customers in the restaurant. In fact, nearly every seat was occupied. A tight grimace crossed his lips, as he hadn't noticed the people when he entered.

A cup of coffee appeared between his hands. Steam floated from the quivering black liquid.

To his right, several seats and patrons away, a coin bounced on the linoleum countertop. It spun and rolled on its edge. Gabe idly watched the dime as it settled to one side, then fell flat.

"You win," a surly voice growled.

Surreal spikes of pain jolted through Gabe. Charlie Harris slid off a stool. Gabe bolted out the exit.

He fumbled with the key at the entrance to his apartment building. "Gabe? You okay?"

He jammed the key into the lock and twisted his wrist. The door opened with Charlie inches away. Gabe slammed the door closed and ran up the stairs two steps at a time. He managed to open the door to his room.

Gabe leaned his back on the wooden door. He slid to the floor and drew his knees up. Wrapping his arms around his shins, he pulled them in tight, buried his head against his knees, and cried.

RELENTLESS knocks at the door woke Gabe. "Go away," he snarled from the bed.

"Gabriel Kasper, you open this door right now."

"Betty?" he stuttered and sat upright. "I—I mean, Mrs. Brewer?"

"Yes, it's Betty. Now open this door, young man."

He cringed. She was using her I-am-so-disappointed-and-furious-with-you tone. He rolled off the bed and shuffled across the floor. Taking a deep breath, he turned the doorknob. She pushed her way past him. An odor of warm custard and baby powder trailed the elderly but energized woman's movements.

"Why don't you get a bigger apartment? How about one with a kitchen? You can afford one, you know." She plopped down on the couch and unwrapped the aluminum foil covering the bowl in her hands. From her coat pocket, she produced a spoon. Betty glowered at him. "Come eat this while it's warm."

Gabe crossed his arms but did as told. He sat beside her and accepted the bowl and spoon. The smell of baby powder stayed with her. The aroma of custard drifted up from the bowl in his hand.

"I'm not really hungry." He knew the point wouldn't be acceptable to her and scooped a spoonful of the thick custard, making sure to include some of the cinnamon dusted across the top.

"So I heard."

He glanced at her out of the corner of his eye. "Who tattled?"

"Gert at the restaurant called me." She patted his thigh. "When you didn't want fried chicken, she knew something was wrong." Betty reached up and gently touched the bump on his noggin. "What is going on with you, Gabriel?"

He savored the flavor of the warm homemade dessert, allowing it to drizzle down his throat. The custard warmed his belly. Her attention warmed his soul.

"Nothing. I tripped and fell on the sidewalk."

She meticulously brushed his hair with her hand while she studied his face like a surgeon. He shifted uncomfortably on the couch.

"You're not telling me the truth." She pulled his head to her and kissed the owie. "Talk to me, Gabriel. What is troubling you?" Her eyelids went to half-mast. "Is it that Mr. Harris in 412? Did he do this to you?"

"No!" he blurted out before he could stop the exclamation. His face and ears burned with embarrassment. He sucked on his lower lip.

Betty took control of the spoon, refilled it, and eased a bite between his lips. He chuckled at her and at his willingness to allow her to mother him. He sloshed the custard into liquid before swallowing. She prepared another spoonful but paused.

"So, who did this to you?"

There would be no avoiding her. She'd never leave until he answered.

"Perkins."

Her cheeks went crimson and her nostrils flared. "I'll slap that boy into next week. He has no business manhandling you. Why did he hit you?" She thrust her hands together, her body shook in her anger, custard dribbled from the edge of the clutched spoon. "I babysat that boy. He wasn't worth a fig then either. Nasty little brat. Broke two wooden spoons on his bare bottom, I did."

Gabe stifled a laugh at the image of the police chief laid out over Betty's knees, getting his butt tanned. Then reality checked in and cancelled his mirth. He looked down at the bowl and let go a heavy sigh.

"It's all over Charlie." He transferred his gaze to Betty. "Mr. Harris."

Her eyes bulged in surprise. "You two were fighting over a man? Howard is a homosexual?" She rattled her head. "I would have never guessed."

This laugh he couldn't suppress. It leapt right out of him.

"Well. I can still coax a smile out of you." She took the bowl and set it on the floor. Tender hands pulled him to her and guided his head to her shoulder. "Talk to me, Gabriel."

An arthritic hand stroked his cheek. He could see the wrinkles in her skin and the bumps on her knuckles. But the love and concern flowing from her hadn't tempered since the day she'd come to the hospital and taken him home with her after the doctors pronounced his parents dead on arrival from the car accident. He'd been sixteen then. Betty had attended his high school graduation and stood and applauded when he received his diploma. She'd been the only person in the gymnasium to do so. He joined the army on his eighteenth birthday. When he came back home, it was Betty who convinced the Larson family to turn over management of the hotel to Gabe.

His chest quivered and jerked. Tears welled. First one rolled down his cheek, then a torrential downpour followed. "I think I'm in love with him."

She leaned in and kissed away the tears.

"Tell Betty all about it," she whispered.

Gabe sucked in two quick breaths and surrendered to her wishes.

Minutes later, when he finished his confession, his priestess glowed with a warm confidence that eased all his pain and insecurities.

"Do what that rapscallion Perkins wants done. And tell no one. No one, I say." She sandwiched his face with her weathered hands. "I'll take care of the rest."

CHAPTER 16

CHARLIE stepped out of the narrow shower and grabbed the towel off a hook to wipe his body dry. The bruise on his thigh already had faint yellow and green striations. He jabbed a finger at the injury. The pain was dull, it wouldn't be a problem. Content with the appraisal, he wrapped the towel around him and returned to his room.

He scrubbed the towel over his hair, then tossed the piece of linen to the floor and lay on the bed. Hands under his head, he closed his eyes and thought about Gabe.

He'd wanted to talk to him, to find out exactly what had happened with Perkins. Now, just as quick as snapped fingers, Gabe had run from him like he had polio.

"What the hell was that about?"

A shot of concern buzzed into his brain, but, curiously, not that Gabe had turned on him. Not a drip of doubt stained his unblemished trust of the man. The picture was safe with Gabe—that's all there was to it. And that's what troubled him. Why didn't he worry Gabe had become too afraid, decided it safer to remain buried in his and this town's secrets? He smacked his lips to interrupt the bewilderment. In a few hours, he had a date with a thief. The reunion would come as a complete surprise to one of them.

Charlie grinned and rolled onto his unbruised side.

ALONGSIDE a wooden fence next to a blank wall of the brick building, Charlie huddled in the darkness between two garbage cans. Fog was rolling in from the river. He turned up his collar and settled a little deeper into his coat. Silver particles swirled and twirled to unheard melodies under the lone lamppost. He pondered the dance. Did dust get moist in fog, and that was the troupe, or did fog carry its own version of the Radio City Rockettes wherever it traveled? The car dealership's multicolored banners hung as limp as they had the night he arrived in town.

He entertained himself by identifying the various levels of stink. Grease and oil seemed to control the bass section. Banana peels, always a crowd pleaser, merged with some rotting lettuce and peanut butter to complete the brass. He contemplated the absence of any detectable jellies. Surely peanut butter would have fruity accompaniment. But, alas, not in this night's concerto of the discarded. A gathering crescendo of tobaccos, both smoking and chaw, vied for lead in the strings.

Charlie tapped his baton finger on his make-believe music stand, surveyed the orchestra with the same studied eye as his old junior high school music teacher, and—

Scrape. Clunk. Click-thunk. Click-thunk. Click-thunk.

Ahh. The percussionist had arrived.

Charlie pushed to his feet and casually walked around the corner. Johnny Upton, with his back to the building, and Charlie, was busy jacking up the rear end of a Chevy.

The moron needed four tires after Charlie had slashed his. Midnight shopping seemed the thief's only option.

"I hope you brought the right lug wrench, dipstick."

Johnny leaned right to rabbit. Charlie grabbed the collar of the leather jacket and yanked the kid backward to the ground. He drew back a fist. Johnny's hands covered the bandages on his face.

"No! Oh, God, please don't. Doc said if I break it again, I might never be able to breathe through my nose ever."

The voice was thick and throaty. Gauze peeked out the nostrils under the wrap. Charlie grabbed the punk by the coat and pulled him to his feet. He moved his grip to the collar and dragged Johnny along beside him.

"Where we going?" Johnny squirmed to free himself.

Charlie slapped the back of the greasy skull, then wiped his hand clean on the black leather jacket.

"City hall."

"Why?"

"I want to break in to the mayor's office. Figured you were the right guy for the job."

Johnny dug the heels of his pointy black shoes into the gravel. "The mayor's office? Oh, shit. Perkins'll kill me."

Charlie spun and thwacked a knuckle on Johnny's gauzed nose.

"Ow!"

"I hadn't really planned on telling him about it, but"—he popped the nose again—"it's up to you. I can splatter your face all over the parking lot right here if you prefer."

Johnny's hands cupped the bandages. "Jesus Christ, mister. What's your problem?"

"Look, punk." Charlie heaved an exasperated breath. "You help me get in the mayor's office, and you can come back here and steal all the tires you need for your convertible. I don't care. Not my cars. Are we communicating yet?" He raised a fist so Johnny couldn't miss the protruding knuckle.

"Yeah. Yes!" Johnny shrugged. "Haven't broken in to city hall before. Sounds pretty hip, Daddy-O."

Charlie popped a knuckle against the protecting hands.

"Jesus! I said yes. What the hell *is* your problem?"

"Let's stick to one language. I only speak English." He turned and pulled Johnny along, stride for stride.

"Okay, okay. Where's your car?"

Charlie kept walking. "Don't have one. Cab's probably not a good idea. Wouldn't exactly trust whoever dropped you off, either."

"That's ten, twelve blocks from here."

"Yeah. Next time you get the urge to steal something, think about a pair of Keds."

THEY waited in the shadows up the side street from city hall. A half hour passed before the cop came out and locked the front door. He got in the squad car and drove away.

"Alley," Johnny said.

Charlie let the kid lead the charge. They walked across the intersection as if they were two buddies out for a drink. Johnny's calmness impressed Charlie. The kid was a loser and no doubt always would be, but he knew his business.

They turned into the alley. Johnny sized up the back of the building.

"I can probably get this door open, but since nobody uses it—"

"How can you tell?" Charlie had become the student.

Johnny ran a hand over the edges and displayed his dirty palm. "Wouldn't be this much dirt if people were going in and out of it. The patrol cop would notice right away if we went in through here. Cops know this stuff too. Same with the first-floor windows."

The thief kicked the latch on the coal chute and it dropped open.

"We can slide in through here, if you don't mind getting covered in coal dust. But the cop would kind of notice us walking down the street. Most folks don't smear their faces with coal before going out on a night on the town."

"Okay. Keep talking, Houdini."

Johnny slid aside a garbage can and pointed. "Basement window. Everybody sets garbage cans in front of them so nobody will think there's a window there."

He turned his back to the wall and kicked backward. Glass tinkled. Wood splintered. The kid sat on his butt and kicked away any remnants of the window. He pushed off with his hands and slid into the building.

Johnny's voice echoed a bit, like he was in a big empty space. "Pull the can back where it was so if the cop drives by he won't see the window's gone."

Half in, half out, Charlie grabbed the can and let its weight gently lower him to the floor. He adjusted the can's position so only the metal container was visible looking out, figuring the reverse would hold true from the outside as well.

"Got a light?"

Charlie dug the matchbook from his pocket and scratched a match across the striker. The sulfur tip hissed and flamed. The room had piles and piles of boxes, dust-covered broken furniture, and a couple file cabinets. The air, amidst the coal stench, was musty, moldy, and damp.

Johnny tapped Charlie's arm. "Stairs."

They walked over and climbed the steps. At the top was a closed door. Charlie blew out the match before it burned him. The darkness swallowed the man next to him.

"Won't the door be locked?"

A click, and the door opened. A channel of dull light sliced the pitch.

"Yeah. From the other side. People lock basement doors so nobody can get into the basement, but they keep the basement side unlocked so they don't lock themselves in. Stupid, huh?"

"Apparently. But what if it had been locked?"

"Kick it open. It's not like anybody's here."

They entered the entryway. Johnny stalled, staring at the door to the police department.

"I've always wanted to break in there. Just so I could say I did it."

Charlie slapped the back of the kid's head and once again wiped the hair grease on the jacket. "That's your whole problem. You talk too much. Come on."

They jogged up the stairs to the door to the mayor's office. Johnny pulled out his switchblade. *Click*. The blade sprang into place. The thief wiggled the blade between door and jamb, then smiled and pushed the door open.

Charlie led the way. He grabbed the doorknob to Roger's private office, but it was locked as well. He waved Johnny forward.

In two shakes of a lamb's switchblade, they were inside.

Gray light through open curtains veiled the room. The paneling was the same as in Roger's office at the Nugget. In a corner were a round table and three chairs. The desk was large. A leather-clad chair sat empty behind the desk. Various pictures of Roger and Dora and people Charlie had no idea who they were adorned the walls. Two bookshelves were packed with books and municipal awards. A door to the right of the desk had a hasp and combination lock sealing it shut.

"So, what are we looking for?"

Charlie put his hands on his hips and stared at the padlocked door. "Not sure. But I'm guessing it's in there."

Johnny grabbed the lock with one hand and gingerly turned the dial with the other. A faint click, and he pulled the lock open and grinned.

"Habit. People are always in a hurry, so they tend to leave the combination ready for the last number. All I ever have to do is turn the dial until it opens. They make this shit so easy."

"Obviously," Charlie growled. "Or you couldn't do it." He pulled the door open. "There's probably loose change in the desk drawers. Help yourself."

Johnny plopped down in the chair and swiveled back and forth. "Hey! Look at me. I'm the mayor!"

Charlie reared back to slap the greasy head again, but he'd gotten a little tired of wiping his hand clean, so he grabbed the kid's ear and twisted instead. "Shut up."

"Ow! Jesus! Okay, okay."

Charlie turned his attention to the room behind the door. It was a closet lined with shelves. He took a step back to allow the dim light to reveal anything worth looking at. Little by little his vision adjusted, but the darkness was still too black. He thumbed a match across the striker of the matchbook and held the flame high. Orange flickered across books, small boxes, piles of paper, and a pottery umbrella stand with four tall rolled up papers. Three were blue. He grabbed one.

Wood scraped over wood—a desk drawer slid open.

"Dang! The mayor must not like to carry change in his pockets. There's gotta be at least three bucks worth here."

"Glad it's a profitable night for you." Charlie hoped the sarcasm wasn't lost on Johnny, but he sensed three dollars in change might be a major score for the tin cup thief.

Charlie unrolled the blueprint on the corner table.

"What you got there?"

Charlie, hands on the ends, studied the white lines. "Not sure."

"Holy shit." Johnny's head popped into view. Charlie turned slightly to minimize the stench of the hair gel. "What do you put in your hair? Axle grease?"

"If that's all I've got. This is for the nuclear power plant."

Charlie's eyes opened wide. This punk knew how to read blueprints? "How do you know that?"

Johnny tapped at the bottom right corner. "Says so."

Charlie's ears burned. "Oh." *Whistle Pass Nuclear Power Station Proposed Site Construction.* He let go of one end. The plans rolled themselves up. He returned that set to the umbrella stand and opened another. Different diagram, same identifying label. The third, same label, different lines. He grabbed the plain paper roll and spread it over the table.

This one was a plot map with red and green lines sketching out locations of where the plant would be erected. Broken yellow lines, along with handwritten notations, revealed the area was to be annexed into the town of Whistle Pass itself.

In the corner label box with jargon and numbers Charlie couldn't decipher sat the property owner's name—Dora Hamilton.

Now, that can't be just a coincidence. He let the paper roll over itself and stuck it back in the umbrella stand.

The nuclear plant was much more than a concept or ideal Roger was working toward. The darn thing was ready to be built once Roger got elected and pushed through an agreement with the state. And... on his wife's land, no less. There had to be tons of money at stake, with a major chunk of it going in Roger's and Dora's pockets.

So what are these two fighting about? There should be more than enough cash to go around.

Unless Dora didn't want the plant built. Charlie scratched at his stubble. But that didn't make sense either. She'd seemed protective of Roger to an extent. Charlie doubted Roger could have even tried to make a run for the state office without her support.

He shook his head. This didn't add up. Dora probably wanted the plant as much as Roger.

Charlie was back to square one.

A drawer slid shut. He looked over to Johnny, who shrugged his disappointment.

"Nothing else worth taking."

"Let's go. How do we get out of here?"

Johnny led the way to the stairs. "Front door. There's a turn knob. We just walk out. The cop'll think he forgot to lock it."

"I thought you said you never broke in here before?"

"Yeah." Their hurried steps echoed around them. "I haven't. But I never said I hadn't planned to."

Charlie chuckled. Old Johnny wasn't just a loser, he was an adrenaline addict, with burglary his fix.

The lock clicked. Johnny pushed open the door and stuck his head outside. "Clear."

Charlie followed the kid out the door.

Johnny wore a massive grin. "That was fun. When you want to break in somewhere else, let me know."

"Keep your mouth shut if you want to keep your nose." Charlie smiled. "You did good. Go get your tires."

Johnny winked and jogged across the street, where he disappeared into the fog and shadows.

Charlie headed for the hotel. The fog blanketed him like smoke—gun smoke. His nostrils flared. The bitter smell of gunpowder crawled into his brain. A car passed by on the street. The exhaust backfired, a mortar round exploded. A bat after an insect strafed his head—*hand grenade*!

"Run, men, run! Take cover!"

"No, LT!" Charlie screamed. "Stay low until we know where the ambush is coming from."

But they didn't listen. They broke and ran. The LT fell. The sergeant fell. Roger, Gabe….

Gabe?

Charlie blinked and looked around. When his nostrils and mind cleared, he was back on Main Street in Whistle Pass. He looked across the street. There stood the hotel, the restaurant, and the door to Gabe's building. He shifted his gaze upward to the two windows—the windows to Gabe's apartment.

He held out his hands. They didn't tremble. Not so much as a twitch.

Wrapping himself in his arms, he listened to his steady, controlled breaths. Gabe Kasper had pulled him back from his insanity. He inhaled the imagined scent of Gabe's Aqua Velva. An image of Gabe's handsome face went straight to Charlie's heart, which pumped the warm vision through his body. He looked back up at the pair of windows. Emptiness gnawed in his chest.

He missed the man's company.

Charlie shoved his hands in his pockets and walked home to room 412 and a long, lonely night of dreaming about Gabe.

FROM the security of his bed, Gabe stared at the ceiling.

He hissed a forlorn breath through clenched teeth. In less than twenty-four hours, he would betray Charlie Harris with a kiss.

He groaned and rolled onto his side, away from the windows. This was going to be the longest night of his life.

CHAPTER 17

FROM the audible ends of the channel, two unseen craft performed a whistle pass.

The fog, thick as smoke, clung to Gabe like his sullen mood. He tugged down the brim of the fedora and used it to break a path through the dampness to the restaurant.

Upon Gabe's opening the door, a very cheery Cathy threw her arms around him and planted a wet one on his cheek.

"Morning, handsome. What are you doing up so early? You don't have to be at work for another two hours."

She pulled a napkin from her apron, and Gabe scrubbed off the lipstick. He scowled at the pink stain.

"Here, grumpy"—she took the napkin from him, spit on it, and rubbed his skin—"let me do it."

He studied the glow of her face and the crystalline liveliness of her eyes. He hadn't seen her this happy and satisfied since she couldn't wait to tell him about her first orgasm. *Shit!*

"Oh, don't tell me. You served Lester breakfast too?" Gabe was no prude, but certain things just shouldn't be done. Clearly, a line had been crossed, and he took no pleasure in having played an instrumental role. "With Richie in the house?"

Her nose touched his—her brows and eyes crossed.

"Richie asked if Lester could spend the night." She leaned back. TNT couldn't have chipped the smile. "What was I to do?" A giggle erupted, and she playfully slapped Gabe's chest. "We played Uncle

Wiggily and slept on the floor in a tent Lester and Richie made from quilts."

Gabe watched her mouth scrunch in… disappointment?

"Richie slept between us."

Cathy studied Gabe's face. The intensity of her gaze shoved his aside.

"Did you sleep at all last night?"

"No." He walked over to an empty table along the wall and sat. "Can I just get some coffee?"

Cathy scurried to the counter and returned with a mug of coffee and an orange, which she promptly peeled with a paring knife, then ticked out the seeds with the tip of the blade. The sweet tart perfume of the peelings wet his mouth.

"No arguments. You need your vitamins." She stuck a wedge between his lips, then swept the orange husks and seeds into her hands and strode off.

He sucked the juice from the slice and mashed the pulp with his back teeth. The chair across from him slid out as he swallowed, and he had to wage war against the urge to hurl. Charlie sat down, his face shaded under a thickening layer of facial fur.

An erotic desire to shave the man from his ears to his thighs pulsed through Gabe.

"We need to talk, but not here." Charlie plucked a wedge of orange from the table. "You mind?"

Fearing what might come out of his mouth, Gabe merely shook his head.

Charlie slid the orange between those thin, sexy lips and chewed. Gabe watched every movement of his jaw and cheeks, and then his throat when Charlie swallowed.

Compose, Gabriel. Compose. He might not be who you want him to be.

The thought snapped Gabe back to the reality of the day and the tasks before him. His hands trembled. He dragged them off the table onto his lap. Gabe focused on the coffee's steam.

"Talking isn't a good idea right now." He didn't want to talk to Charlie, but he couldn't rebuke the man either. His left hand played finger tag with the right. "I—I...." He nervously filled his lungs. He needed to have faith in Betty. She'd saved him when his folks died. She'd save him now. He just needed to trust her. The words rushed out in his exhaled breath. "I have a really busy day. How about we get together in the park by the river tonight. Eight okay?"

"Sure." Charlie stood.

Fear rattled through Gabe. He crossed his arms and grabbed his shoulders. The steam spun in the cup, taunted Gabe in his deception with a vapor. *Liar*. He blasted a breath across the coffee. The small cloud fell off the side of the mug, only to reform and continue its silent chimney of accusations.

"See you then." Charlie walked away. A slap of chilly air struck Gabe's neck as the door opened and closed.

Gabe gripped his hands together. His breaths turned fast and shallow, and somehow the fog outside seeped into his brain. Darkness closed over his eyes.

Crinkling paper covered his mouth. He swiped at it, but hands slapped his away.

"Breathe in and out. Deep, Gabe. Breathe." Cathy's voice slipped into a void and echoed in chasms in his head. "You're hyperventilating. Breathe. That's it. Slow. Steady."

The paper bag filled and collapsed in time with his breaths. He blinked as he watched the sack. His lungs rallied and slowed. He nodded, and the bag disappeared.

"Come on." She pulled him from the chair. "You need to lie down for a while." He leaned on her as they walked. "I'll be right back," she said to the air.

The cold and damp roused him further. His shuffling became steps. Cathy pushed open the hotel's door. Betty scurried over.

"What happened?"

"He saw Charlie. Got to admit, the man is good-looking. If you like your men rough, tough, and hairy."

Gabe scolded her with a side glance. She patted his gaze forward with an open palm. "I'm just saying you have good taste." She passed him off to Betty. "But he could use a shave."

An image surfaced of Charlie's naked body under Gabe's razor. He rolled his eyes and groaned.

Arm over Betty's shoulders, he let her lead the way to the back room, where he stretched out on the sofa. She spread a blanket over him, then kissed his forehead.

"You get some rest. I told you I'll take care of it, and I meant it." She kissed him again. The wrinkled lips on his skin were old slippers and flannel PJs to his soul.

Comforted by Betty's presence, he closed his eyes. Under her motherly watch the world outside and the events he seemed to have no control over minimized and became almost tolerable, manageable. She would protect him, just like she always had. Betty had never let him down, and she wouldn't now.

He quickly fell asleep.

GABE jogged to the doors of the stone courthouse and glanced at the iron penile erection on the corner, publicly referred to as the Mount Robertson city clock. The first of ten scheduled dongs tolled. He jerked the door open and entered. An occasional board creaked under his hurried steps. Lester waited in the hall.

"Think I wasn't coming?" Gabe asked to break his guilt for cutting the ten o'clock appointment so close.

Lester shrugged. "No. You said you'd be here, so I knew you would." He turned a blemished doorknob and pushed the solid wooden door open.

An old paper and ink musk smacked Gabe in the nose. He rested his arms on the chest high counter.

"Be right with you," the old man bent over a table said. Under the glare of a green glass-shaded desk lamp, the man ran a finger along lists in a book the size of an open newspaper. Rows of perpendicular cabinets housed dozens of similar sized books.

The fingertip tapped at something on the page. "Found it." The finger went to the round gold eyeglasses on the bridge of his long nose and slid the frames to the top. He scribbled on a notepad. Grabbing a cane dangling by its curved handle from the table, the man hobbled to the counter, where he tore off the page he'd written on and handed it to Lester, who gave it to Gabe.

"I came over after I dropped Richie at school and asked Mr. Olson to check for you." Lester lowered his head. "You mad?"

Gabe smiled at his brute of a friend's shy and demure side. "No. I appreciate your thinking of me." He looked at the paper. *Bad River Timber Company, Odanah, Wis.*

His head throbbed. Odds were better than a sure thing Charlie worked for the electric company by way of this logging firm. A pang of jealousy mixed with his confusion and frustration. The recipe cooked up little doubt Charlie was in town to take care of a problem for the mayor. With the police chief wanting Charlie served on a platter— Gabe heaved a troubled sigh—the mayor's wife had to be the problem.

A new thought set a muscle in his jaw twitching. Just how did Charlie plan on taking care of Dora? On impulse, he covered his mouth with an open hand. Murder? Was Charlie a killer for hire?

Compose, Gabriel. Compose. You've seen way too many movies.

He wanted to get out of here, find Charlie, and talk to him. This whole situation was getting way out of control. Yes, he trusted Betty, but she didn't have experience in stuff like this. He frowned at himself. Neither did he. Maybe the time had come to stop depending on other people, to stop dreaming of a better life… to stop hiding and step up to the plate as a man. A man like Charlie Harris.

Oh, God. Could he have a thought that didn't have Charlie at its epicenter?

A rustle of paper drew his attention. Lester spread a map across the countertop and looked at Gabe. "I had time on my hands, so I grabbed a map at the service station."

Gabe appreciatively patted Lester's immense and hard-as-a-rock shoulder. "Thanks." Lester'd thought this out a lot more than Gabe had. He checked the index for Odanah, found the letters and numbers to locate the town on the map, then dragged his fingers from each starting point until they met. A tiny circle and *Odanah* rested below his touch.

"What's this shaded area?"

Lester tapped the paper. "Indians." He fingered a line under some faint letters across the light gray the town sat on the edge of. *Bad River Ojibwe Reservation.*

Gabe's brow wrinkled as he squinted in thought. Charlie was an Indian? How? He muffled a slight chuckle. *How, heap big chief Charlie.* He shook off the inappropriateness of the sarcasm. Besides, Charlie wasn't an Indian. Indians couldn't grow beards. Could they? None of them he saw in the movies had beards, or shaved. The pioneers in the wagon trains always shaved with straight razors dipped into wooden water barrels strapped to the side of a wagon, but he couldn't recall Indians ever shaving. The Indians on the linen postcards he'd seen never had beards. Or a moustache, for that matter.

He sucked in his cheeks. *No. Charlie's no Indian.* Satisfaction settled his disconcertedness. There was just no way he could be in love with an Indian, of all things.

"Shame on you." Lester spun and walked out the door that clicked closed behind him.

Gabe tried to fold the map, failed miserably, and crumpled it under his arm. "Thanks, Mr. Olson." Using Lester's heavy footfalls as a guide, he ran down the hall. He caught him at the front doors.

"What? What'd I do?"

The scowl on the big man knotted the muscles in Gabe's butt.

"I saw your face. You think the logging man might be an Indian." Eyelids lowered, the deep-set eyes hazed. "You aren't any different than those boys in school who made fun of you." Lester stomped down the sidewalk.

"Me?" Lester wasn't making any sense at all. "I'm not a bigot!" But Lester continued walking. "Damn it, Lester. I'm a queer, for crying out loud! How could I be a bigot?"

An approaching couple stepped into the grass to go around him. The pink-coated woman grabbed the suited man's arm. The man frowned and placed his left arm across his chest as if to ward off some contagious evil spirit.

Gabe raised his hands in the air, waggled his fingers, and opened his eyes until they hurt. "Boogity, boogity."

The couple scurried to the courthouse doors. The man threw one open, glanced back at Gabe, and hustled inside behind the woman.

Oh, good move, Gabriel. The sheriff's office is on the other side of the building.

He ran full stride for the DeSoto. Gabe Kasper needed to get the hell out of Dodge—or rather, in this case, Mount Robertson.

CHAPTER 18

CHARLIE sipped coffee in the newsstand until the mayor entered city hall. He ground out his cigarette in the ashtray and walked to the counter, where he pulled out his change holder, removed a dime, and slapped the coin on the countertop to pay for the brew. Returning the red rubber holder to his pocket, he grabbed a loose coin in his jeans pocket.

"Heads, you win, tails, you lose." He spun the second dime.

The man behind the counter intently watched the revolving metal. "This for my tip again?"

"Yup." Charlie absently pulled out another cigarette and lit it from a matchbook. He looked out the windows. The fog had lifted somewhat. Maybe the day wouldn't be too bad after all. The edges of the coin rattled as it settled.

"Damn." The man snapped his fingers in disappointment.

"Tails, you lose." Charlie picked up the dime, stuffed it back in his pocket, and walked outside. He turned left, as if to head for Captain Tom's a few blocks up. There was a phone booth along the route. Hopefully, old Dora wouldn't mind a morning phone call.

A BIG Buick pulled to the curb. Charlie glanced at the empty backseat and floor. *Time to milk the rattlesnake.* He opened the front passenger door and climbed in. Pungent perfume scoured the lining of his nose.

"Did you really think I would try and hide someone in the back?" Dora Black asked as she drove the car down the street.

He tilted his head. "Never know. I'm guessing you're capable of a lot of things."

"That I am, Mr. Harris." Her scarf-covered head turned slightly toward Charlie, but under the black oversized lenses of the sunglasses, he couldn't tell if she'd looked at him or not. The tightly knit pink wool coat and blue cotton dress gave her the appearance of a mom running a forgotten errand. "Including whatever I have to do to protect my husband."

There, she'd said it again. At the steakhouse she'd said she was protecting Roger too. He scratched at his beard. The meeting request had been to make sure he hadn't misunderstood or didn't correctly remember what she'd said. A muscle in his chest jerked.

If these two, Dora and Roger, were really at war, why protect Roger? And why, of all people, from Charlie?

He raised a finger toward her. "You really think no one will recognize you in the disguise?"

She grabbed at a flat silver case between them on the seat, fumbling it with her fingers. The metal case slid to the floor. Charlie leaned over, picked it up, then snapped open the lid. Old Dora enjoyed a bit of tobacco. It was a cigarette case.

Charlie pulled out one of the Philip Morris smokes, stuck it in his mouth, and lit it from his matchbook. She handed him an ivory-colored holder. He twisted the cigarette into the long stem and offered it back to her.

Dora inhaled, then, head tilted back, released the smoke in a slow stream to the ceiling.

"Thank you, Mr. Harris." The voice remained a dull monotone.

"It's okay to call me Charlie," he said in an attempt to melt the frozen witchcicle.

"Mr. Harris, I agreed to this sordid little summit because you said you had something important to tell me. Say it, give me the photograph, or get out." A finger tapped the steering wheel. "The car's borrowed. No one will recognize me."

Charlie raised a brow. Had a breach been made in the embattlements?

Her right hand went in her coat pocket. She pulled out just enough of the object for Charlie to see the wooden grip of a pistol. "So, if I need to kill you before I go home and prepare supper, no one will have seen us together."

He gulped. A breach? Not an ice cube's chance on a July rooftop. Old Dora was nobody to screw with—Charlie risked an amused grin—unless she chose to spread her legs, of course. She'd probably made her money charging toll between her thighs.

"Half a mile up this road there is an entrance to some backwater docks. You have until then to say what you came to say."

Okay. You want to play? He'd thrown a dart at Roger and hit pay dirt, no reason he couldn't continue his lucky streak.

"I think your devoted husband wants me to kill you."

Dora slumped in the seat. Her hands dropped to her sides.

"Oh shit!"

The car's front tire bumped the highway curb, and the car bounced and careened across the centerline. Charlie dove for the freewheeling steering wheel. The beast shuddered against the curb on the other side of the roadway and the ton and a half rolling piece of steel chugged toward the opposite highway edge.

"Oh, Jesus. Don't you die on me, Dora." Pressed against the still woman, Charlie jerked the wheel left, then right. The car's path straightened. He palmed the gearshift upward, it clunked into neutral, and he guided the car along the roadway while it steadily slowed.

"Don't you die, Dora. Oh, Jesus Christ. Don't you die."

Charlie stretched his left leg to the brake and repeatedly pumped the pedal to slow the car even more.

"Breathe, Dora. You can do it." Her body slipped to the door, her head on the ledge at the base of the window. He shot a glance to her still face and parted lips. "Breathe, Goddamn you!"

A field entrance appeared to the right, and Charlie turned the wheel. The Buick coasted to a stop at the gate. He stretched his leg to the emergency brake and kicked the pedal. It ratcheted to the floor.

Charlie tugged the unconscious woman upright. He pulled off her sunglasses. Her blue eyes glistened. She casually blinked her elongated eyelashes.

"You can go back to your side of the car now, Mr. Harris." Dora snatched the sunglasses out of his hand and returned them to her eyes. "Unless you're not a homosexual, in which case, maybe we should move this party to the backseat."

Stunned but relieved, Charlie leaned back. "You were faking?"

On the one hand, possibly the left, he was so damn glad to see her alive, he wanted to kiss her. On the other hand, definitely the right, as it had balled to a fist, he wanted to knock the bitch out.

"Mr. Harris."

A boot up her ass would probably render nothing more than a bored yawn.

"*Mr. Harris.* Return to your seat or remove your jeans. I'm not kidding. I admit to more than a lurid and morbid curiosity as to whether you could satisfy me the way you apparently once satisfied my husband." The glacier eyes moved with a glacier's speed. "Do you happen to know where my cigarette holder went to?"

The lifeless gaze bored into every bone in Charlie's spine. His mind quivered at the awareness she'd found a crack to ooze inside him.

"You're nuts." He scooted to the passenger side of the car. "You're out of your mind."

Charlie settled in his seat and stared out the window at a solitary black and white cow idly watching the show from beyond the closed gate. He dug in a coat pocket for his Luckies. The shaking in his hand knocked one out of the pack far enough he could grab the tobacco stick between his teeth.

He ripped a paper match out of the book. The sulfur head crumbled on the striker.

Click. Phssh. A smell of lighter fluid filled the car. The flame appeared above a silver lighter in Dora's hand.

"Allow me."

Charlie managed to spear the flame with the cigarette and pulled in a drag. He exhaled around the cigarette clamped in his mouth. The tip bounced up and down.

"I'm not sorry, Mr. Harris. Not in the least. When you said my husband wanted you to kill me, I needed to know if that was in fact your intention here today." A chuckle fell on his ear. "Obviously, it wasn't." A knuckle scraped his cheek. "It really is a pity, you know. We could have had such a marvelous time together." She adjusted herself in the driver's seat and lit her cigarette on the end of the holder.

Charlie rolled down the window. Smoke flowed in a wave out the gap. The chill of damp air calmed his nerves. It wasn't the forest, but he didn't have anything else.

A bolt of heat burned through his core. He hadn't slipped into shellshock. Not so much as a rifle shot had risen in his brain. Not a scream, not a single toothpick of need to charge into hell and fight the devil.

Gabe's face floated across his mind's eye. Charlie rubbed the hair on his chin. *Gabe*. He smiled. The man had affected, or, maybe, infected him. A mild laugh thumped his chest. Either way, Gabe Kasper had changed him.

"Care to share what has amused you?"

"No." He turned his back to the door. "Want to talk?"

Dora pulled the Philip Morris out of the holder and snubbed the embers out in the ashtray. She leaned against the driver's door. "Tit for tat. You're my guest." She held out her palm. "Please."

Charlie genuinely grinned at Dora. Psycho didn't begin to describe her, but the woman definitely had her own unique style.

"Why'd you send Perkins to beat up Gabe?"

She ran a finger under her nose. "I didn't. Where's the photograph?"

She didn't send Perkins? The possibility existed she'd decided to lie in this exchange. He wouldn't lie, but he didn't have to tell the whole truth. "Don't have it anymore. Why do you want the picture?"

"So you have nothing to blackmail my husband with. Why are you blackmailing Roger?"

"*Me*? I'm blackmailing Roger?" A lightning jolt straightened his spine. Where'd this nonsense come from?

Dora crossed her arms and drummed the left bicep of her coat. Her gaze cut through Charlie as if he were a frog in a high school lab class.

"That's two questions, and you didn't answer mine. But it appears your questions may be the answer I sought." She stopped the drumming and stroked the bicep. "Interesting situation, is it not, Mr. Harris? It seems we are either dire enemies or reluctant allies."

This was way too strange. He had to get a grip on whatever was happening here. Might as well put it all out on the table.

"I'm not sure whose turn it is."

She flopped open a hand.

"You own a lot of land south of Whistle Pass. Am I right?"

"Yes. Why is that your concern?" She reached up, grabbed the sunglasses, and tossed them onto the dashboard. Her left eye twitched. He'd struck a chord.

"You planning on selling it?"

"No. Why do you want to know?" Both her hands gripped her coat and tugged at it. A scent of salty, damp wool rose from her. Old Dora had broken a sweat under her coat.

The ice queen's façade and concentration were cracking. She hadn't so much as commented on how he didn't answer her question before asking another. Charlie gnashed the awareness and the fact he didn't know why Dora's mask had slipped, between his teeth. "Because I saw the plans for the power plant."

"Get out."

Huh? "We were getting along so well."

"Get. Out. Of the car."

Clearly the land and power plant had hit a nerve. But what kind? And why?

"I'm not blackmailing Roger. Think about it. If I coughed up the picture, I'd have as much to lose as he would."

Dora reached in her pocket and set the pistol, a small revolver, in her lap. Charlie tensed.

"Then why are you here?"

Okay. Dora hadn't sent the telegram either. So, who had? Or were Roger and Dora both lying? "Somebody sent me a telegram to come. I thought it was from Roger."

She pointed to the floor at Charlie's feet. "Would you hand me my cigarette case, please?"

He bent and retrieved the metal case. When he straightened, the gun was in her hand. Pointed at Charlie's head, the barrel had grown to the size of a bazooka. The part of him that kept him alive woke and purred. Charlie flicked his cigarette out the window.

He kept his voice low and serious, but not threatening, so Dora would hopefully understand how close to death she really was. "If Roger's told you anything about me, then you know there isn't a thing that can stop me from killing you once you pull the trigger. It'll happen that fast."

Dora's gaze locked with Charlie's. The woman's resolve didn't budge. Something beyond Charlie's comprehension had hold of the pistol. Whatever it was, to Dora, it was worth dying for. It made her more dangerous than Charlie. He didn't want to kill her, but there might not be another option. He kept his words soft.

"This doesn't have to happen. Maybe we can still help each other."

"Are you telling me the truth about seeing plans for the power plant?"

The damn power plant again. "Yeah. They're in a closet in his office at city hall. Go see for yourself." He didn't share the chuckle rolling around in his chest. Apparently, Roger had a big surprise coming if Dora decided to follow Charlie's suggestion.

Ratch. Click. She'd pulled back the hammer.

The hair on the back of Charlie's neck stood and drilled into his skin. His muscles tightened. His lungs froze. They'd reached the brittle edge of life and death. Dora had the pull of a trigger left to live.

She eased the hammer down with her thumb and lowered the gun.

Charlie pushed the stale air out of his chest in a relieved sigh.

"The land's in my name, but it belongs to my father. If something happens to me before he dies, my will returns the deed to his name." She laid the pistol in her lap. Her fingers rubbed her eyes. "For the plant to be built on our property, I'm not the only one who would have to die, Mr. Harris. My father would never allow his land to be used that way. His great-grandfather first farmed that land." She lowered her hands to her lap and rested them over the revolver. "My husband is the beneficiary in the event of my and my father's deaths, Mr. Harris." A tear rolled down the ice queen's cheek. She visibly ignored it. "Help me, Mr. Harris. Help me keep my father alive."

Shit! Charlie's thoughts twisted to a tornado, destroying any semblance of sanity in its path. He'd tossed out the murder scenario as bait, and a whale had pulled him under. *Shit!*

But it was Roger who'd planted the idea in his head. Maybe Roger had sent the telegram after all. Maybe Roger had manipulated this whole mess in an attempt to convince Charlie to kill Dora.

His emotions jumped aboard the whirlwind. Fear, worry, dread, anger... they all welded together to form a jumbled up ball of lead that rolled to rest in his stomach.

Something hard nestled in his open palm. He closed his hand around it. *Shit!* He looked down at the pistol.

"Kill him, Mr. Harris. Kill my husband before he kills my father."

Charlie's neck muscles melted. His head slapped onto the seat. The beige ceiling cloth slowly came into focus.

Shit.

He jammed index fingers against his throbbing temples and tried to grind the tips through his skull. One semi-sane spark of logic did manage to jump the gap from fingertip to fingertip: Old Dora just might be a lying bitch.

DORA dropped him off in front of Captain Tom's. A beer or twelve sounded damn good. Charlie opened the door and walked into a refrigerator of silence.

Tom stood in front of the bar with Terry and Ted on either side of him. All of the seats at the tables were filled with men in denim, flannel, and a few in camouflage. Every eye trained on Charlie like hounds on a fox.

Charlie's nerves went to stone. His breaths came steady and calm. Through the haze of smoke from smoldering cigars and cigarettes, he scanned the beer-bottle-covered tables. A man in a red cap put a hand in his canvas jacket pocket. So did a bearded guy. A muscle twitched in red cap's cheek. Red cap was nervous. Beard's eyes narrowed, and a corner of his mouth tightened. Beard had killed before. Might be a combat veteran. Beard would have to be taken out first if it came to that. Charlie wrapped his fingers around the pistol in the pocket of his pea coat.

"We're closed," Tom growled and crossed his arms. "Get out."

"Or you need some help finding the door?" Ted slurred the question.

This bunch had been drinking for a while, building up beer muscles for whatever they had planned.

Charlie backed his way to the exit. Reaching behind him, he found the latch and opened the door. He eased out to the sidewalk and walked sideways, just in case a couple of the boys decided to take care of business on the street.

He jogged around the corner, then into the alley where he broke into a full run to put distance between him and the vigilantes. At the next intersection he slowed and looked over his shoulder. Nobody had followed.

He leaned his back against a building and pulled out a cigarette. With his thumb, he scratched a match across the striker. The match flashed in his hand. Something flashed in his mind. He crouched and scanned the area.

"Run, men. Run. Take cover."

"No, LT. Stay low until we know where—" Charlie squinted, clenched his teeth, and yanked Gabe's face to the forefront.

He whirled and waited. But the gunshots, the explosions, the screams, didn't come. Gabe smiled. Charlie smiled back at him and stood.

Charlie watched Gabe wander back to the recesses of Charlie the man inhabited now. He picked his cigarette off the sidewalk and puffed the ember to life.

"Thanks, Gabe."

Charlie looked around to get his bearings. Captain Tom and his little cadre of bigots had something in the works. Based on the less-than-welcome reception in the bar, whatever it was no doubt included Charlie. Which raised the question of why they hadn't taken advantage of him stumbling into the middle of their war council.

The tobacco crackled as he took a long drag. The answer swirled in the smoke he blew out: because it wasn't the right time or place. Charlie took another hit off the cigarette. Time. Place. Where would he be that they might know about so they could ambush him? "Oh, no," he groaned.

The park. Eight o'clock. With Gabe.

He filled his lungs with smoke, then emptied them in an uneasy burst. "Aww, Gabe. What did you do?"

Part of Charlie wanted to slap the shit out of the man. Another part wanted to get on a bus and never look back. But his heart still wanted, still needed, to believe in Gabe.

Charlie stuck the cigarette between his third and fourth fingers so he couldn't drop it while he walked. This town had to be filled with hunters and fishermen. The hardware store should have a wide variety of ammunition for sale that would fit the pistol.

But first he needed to make a call. Surely there was a newspaper in Chicago in need of a good story. He looked down the street for the phone booth.

CHAPTER 19

TING ting ting ting ting.

Gabe slapped the button on the alarm clock. Using his hands as pillows, he stared at the ceiling. He hadn't slept, not a wink, but that hadn't been his intention. He'd taken refuge in his room in the frivolous hope the planet might implode and he wouldn't have to go to the park.

In the bathroom he whipped the round brush's bristles over the slab of hardened cream in the shaving mug while the sink filled with hot water. The rising heat and soapy scent of the lather didn't aid in settling his nerves. The man in the mirror looked as scared as Gabe. Dull pulses of pain twitched in his cheek. He idly watched the tiny uncontrollable jerks of skin. His heart beat out a flamenco rhythm no dancer could keep pace with. He picked up the safety razor and put it to his throat. The silver razor jiggled in his hand.

"Great," he sarcastically muttered. Though the possibility of cutting a jugular carried with it a fraction of a second's peace through suicide, his own death wouldn't resolve the problem. Perkins would still go after Charlie, with or without Gabe.

He opened his mouth and blew a breath against the glass. A mask of fog obscured the face. A death shroud?

As he set the razor down, it clinked on the porcelain sink. He pulled the chain attached to the rubber stopper to drain the water. Better to arrive without blood-encrusted nicks dotting his features. Betrayal deserved to be done while at one's best.

Betrayal.

He jammed his hand into the water and stabbed the stopper back in the drain. The gurgle of escaping water stopped.

Gabe grabbed a towel to wipe the mirror clean. With each stroke the reflection and Gabe's purpose became clearer.

Perkins would go after Charlie with or without Gabe.

He placed his hands on the sink and leaned toward the mirror, staring at the gray eyes staring at him.

Perkins would go after Charlie with or without Gabe.

Betty had understood that. It had to be why she didn't offer any alternatives to going to the park. He'd told Betty he loved Charlie. The reflection smiled in agreement with the epiphany.

Betty was involved because she loved Gabriel. She wasn't about to leave him alone in this situation and would do whatever she had to in order to keep him safe. Tonight wasn't about betrayal. Tonight was about protecting the man he loved.

Police Chief Howard Perkins had screwed up.

Gabe brushed heavy cream over his jaw and chin. He picked up the razor and studied it in his hand. Not a quake or quiver. Gabriel Kasper would be at his man's side for whatever happened tonight. And he'd look damn good doing it.

He glared at the reflection and scraped the razor down his cheek.

GABE carefully seated the fedora on his head to protect his groomed hair and inhaled the night. Exhaust, street oil, a collage of foods from the restaurant, and the fish-laden potpourri of the river served as the flint to ignite a reminder that Whistle Pass had been his life's safety net to this point.

He buttoned his wool coat and lifted his chin in determination. Existing in a cocoon of safety was… safe, but existing wasn't living. His combat-booted feet smacked the concrete as he strode across the street toward the park.

He'd properly attired himself for the unknown. Fedora and dress coat disguised his T-shirt and jeans with rolled cuffs. An outward appearance of propriety blanketed his preparedness for whatever might happen.

His stride carried him alongside the brick wall of Lilly Grant's Bakery and the attached iron fire escape to the pair of railroad tracks. He doggedly walked over the crossing and entered the park. A thick, rolling gauze edged toward the riverbank. A smattering of stars blinked under a sliver of moon. The water's current gently rocked an uncovered rowboat tied with a slack rope to a pier. Subtle pats of slow waves on rocks trickled a tempo for Gabe's footfalls.

Under a lighted lamppost Charlie sat on a bench, legs extended. A small cloud of smoke formed at his mouth and climbed upward. His hand remained at his face. The collar of the pea coat stood straight around his neck. Red embers glowed and painted the man an eerie shade of devil. A flick of his fingers sent the embers somersaulting to the water. He turned toward Gabe. Another cloud of smoke rose out of him.

Acid dripped from tense nerves and sloshed and seared Gabe's stomach, but his gait and resolve didn't lessen.

Charlie pulled in his legs and sat up straight. His hands went in his coat pockets. Yellow light from the lamppost illuminated the man's hair.

Gabe stopped at the end of the bench. Bile shot up his throat. He gulped it down. His muscles shivered. Charlie's chocolate eyes were laced with anger and... sadness?

He knows. Gabe's brain swirled in uncertainty at how to react or feel about this obvious fact.

Charlie tipped his head. "Sit down." His voice, steady, offered no emotion to gauge his true feelings by.

Gabe sat next to the armrest, placing as much distance between them as possible. He intertwined his fingers and rested his hands in his lap. He avoided Charlie's gaze by looking at the lines on the man's forehead and the dangling strand of hair dividing the plows in half.

"How's it supposed to happen?"

"Perkins wants me to kiss you." Gabe's gaze dropped to the hands in his lap. He tapped his index fingertips together. The verbal admission of the betrayal sandpapered his throat raw, cracked his voice. "I'm not sure what's going to happen after that."

He looked into Charlie's eyes and rushed the next words, needing to hear the encouragement as much as offer it. "But it will be all right, Charlie. I swear. It's going to work out."

Charlie blew a smokeless breath between tightened lips. "Yeah? And how do you know that?"

Gabe sighed at how ridiculous the answer would undoubtedly sound to Charlie. But the truth and his reliance on a woman who would sacrifice all for him were all he had to offer. He looked at the stone face.

"Betty's taking care of it."

Charlie's body bounced in a scornful laugh. "The old lady from the hotel?"

The sneering tone rolled Gabe's hands into fists. The left side of his face wrenched, the nostril flared, and anger roiled through him. He nearly screamed his resentment. "Don't talk about Betty like that. You don't know her, Charlie. Betty loved me and took care of me when nobody else gave a shit. Do you have any idea what it's like having someone in your life that you know would risk everything for you? *Do you*, Charlie?"

Charlie was on him before Gabe saw so much as a twitch. Hands squeezed Gabe's face; warm, moist lips covered Gabe's. Charlie's tongue darted between Gabe's lips, traced the tops of his lower teeth, then the upper. The mouth pressed even tighter on his.

Startled, Gabe snorted in air through his nose. Electricity zipped straight from his mouth to his groin. The muscles in his ass convulsed and rolled into balls. His ears flamed to a temperature rivaled only by the intense desire writhing throughout his body.

The powerful hands sandwiching his face pushed his head back an inch or two. Charlie's glistening eyes drilled into his.

"Yeah, I do." His whispered words barely escaped the hot, tobacco-scented breath stroking Gabe's face. "It's why you're here."

He understands! Gabe's hands found the back of Charlie's head. He wrapped locks of thick hair around his fingers and pulled Charlie to him. Gabe's lips captured Charlie's, his tongue thrust inside Charlie's luscious mouth and flicked the tip of his heated tongue.

"Get 'em! Get the queers, boys!"

Shouts and a buffalo herd of footsteps shattered the silence, but not the moment. Charlie pushed away slightly and smiled.

"I'm not too sure I'm not in love with you."

The thunder of his heartbeats filled Gabe's ears. "You… you're in love with—"

A volcanic eruption of pain consumed Gabe's head—a tide of black devoured him whole.

CHAPTER 20

CHARLIE squeezed his eyes tight to ward off the pain. It didn't work. Whatever they'd hit him with left a line of hurt from the crown of his head to his little toes. He turned his head left and brushed against… canvas? He turned his head right. Same coarse material. Breaths of air came hot and hard, difficult to draw. Beads of sweat rolled down his face into his ear. Pitch darkness welcomed the opening of his eyes.

Shit. A hood covered his head. He drew in a deep breath. Air filled with the stench of his salty sweat fought its way through the canvas that sucked against his nose when he inhaled and floated away when he exhaled. Vibration rattled its way inside him. Movement. Wherever, whatever, he was on or in was moving. But slowly, as if the driver was being cautious of the road. Cool air blanketed his body and served to intensify the heat within the hood. He was outside. He flexed his leg muscles, then his pelvic muscles, and finally his shoulders. His body was laid out straight. So, this had to be the back of a truck, not the cramped trunk of a car. Probably a pickup.

One arm was under the right side he was lying on. The other, over his ribs. With his shoulders, he pulled at his arms, tried to bring them around in front of him. They didn't obey. The backs of his hands touched. He rolled and turned his wrists. A scratchy fiber bound them together. Rope. He tried to separate his ankles. Too much tension. Something bound them too. More rope, no doubt. An odd, unfamiliar point of pressure pushed against his right ankle and leg inside his boot. He focused on the pressure. The pistol. The morons hadn't found the pistol. Only a total idiot wouldn't notice the denim over his right boot was much tighter than the left. Unless they were drunk. If this was Captain Tom's bunch of backyard bigots, boozed brains might have overlooked something else as well. Charlie just needed to find it.

He rolled onto his back and scratched at the steel floor. Ribbing. Definitely the bed of a pickup. They wouldn't have left him alone in an open truck bed. There had to be a guard or two.

Charlie stretched, elongated his body as much as he could. The engine whined behind his head. Bumps and bounces of a wheel jiggled stronger to his right. So, his head was toward the cab and he was near a side of the truck, not in the center. These idiots couldn't have put Gabe in the same truck. Could they? Once Charlie learned what it was they really wanted from him, Gabe's life was the only ace these fools had to stop him from tearing them apart, piece by piece.

A brake ground on an axle beneath him. The truck slowed even more, nearly stopped. His weight sloshed left as the truck crept right. A front wheel inched off a slight drop, then the other wheel. The motor revved slightly, and the truck gained speed. Charlie tightened his muscles and braced for the impact.

Thu-thud. The back wheels hit the ground.

Charlie's body bounced; his head banged the floor.

"Ungh," a voice groaned nearby at ear level.

Gabe?

"Jesus Christ! Will you watch it? Terry almost fell out." The surly voice was familiar. And to Charlie's right.

"Oh, thanks, Ted. I thought we weren't supposed to use names?" That voice was to his left.

"Oh, shut your yap. What difference does it make? They can't see us," Ted snarled.

They. Gabe is here. Ted and Terry. Yeah. The familiar voice was Ted from the card game. Charlie slid his legs left. An extended, still leg stopped them. Gabe. The leg quivered, jerked, then pressed against Charlie.

"Charlie? Is that you?" The voice quavered and cracked. "It's going to be all right. I swear it is."

"Yeah, Gabe. It is." Maybe Gabe could afford to place his faith in an old woman and wait for help, but Charlie didn't operate that way. The slumbering beast within him opened an eye, stretched its limbs, and licked its chops. Time to attack the enemy.

A kick to his right knee. "No talking," Ted growled.

Charlie slid his legs right; feet stopped his progression. Both feet pushed against him.

"You best not touch me, queer."

Charlie inched his legs left, then swung them right, under the feet. Ted's feet pressed down on Charlie's lower thigh and upper calf.

"Get your—"

Charlie tensed, then shoved all his strength and will into his waist and legs and flipped them upward. Ted's weight lifted, then was gone.

"Stop the goddamn truck!" Terry screamed. "Ted just fell out!"

Charlie rolled back on his shoulders and slid his tied hands under his butt. He drew in his knees and slipped his hands under his feet, then over his boots to his right ankle. In one swift motion, he pulled up his pants leg and grabbed the pistol. He spun on his ass and fired toward the voice.

"Aiyee!"

The truck skidded to a smooth stop. *Not gravel. Dirt and grass.*

Panicked voices shouted unintelligible words. Other vehicles slid to a halt. Doors snapped open. Charlie yanked off the hood and fired a wild shot in the direction of the truck's cab and then to the rear.

"Charlie?" Gabe shrieked. "Charlie! Are you okay?"

"Yeah. Fine. Stay low." Charlie drew in a breath of cool air, embraced the chilly night against his sweat-covered face. He leaned over and pulled the hood off Gabe. Gabe heavily sucked air. Shadows of men scurried for cover in dense lines of trees on either side of the road.

"Shoot the son of a bitch!" somebody hollered.

"I left the shotgun in the truck. You shoot the son of a bitch," another responded.

Charlie lay down next to Gabe, then poked his head up enough to see over the sides of the truck bed.

"Arnie! You got your pistol?"

Charlie turned left toward the voice.

"Yeah."

Charlie pivoted right, the direction of that voice. "Phil's got his too. We'll get him."

"Don't shoot my damn truck! You don't got a clear shot, wait, for Chrissakes! I'm still making payments!"

Charlie rolled on his side and drew his knees to his chest. With his fingers, he picked at the knot in the rope around his feet. It loosened. He pushed the rope over one boot heel, then the other. At least his legs and feet were free. He turned his attention to Gabe. "Roll on your side so I can untie you."

Gabe scooted onto his left side; Charlie dug at the rope until it gave way. Gabe rolled over and fumbled at the knot binding Charlie's wrists. His breath came short and static. Sweat drenched his features. His perfect hair was flat and matted, glued to his forehead. Hands busy at the rope, his gray eyes blinked fast and heavy in a battle against the sweat in them.

Bang! Zszs. A red comet hissed and wheezed into the sky. A trail of dying, fading sparks of red and white feathered in its wake.

The night went stone quiet. A cricket chirped—a second pair of insect legs rubbed a reply. Charlie watched, stunned, as the flare hit its range, arced, fell limp, and burnt out.

Bang! Zszs. Another screaming ball shot toward the sliver of moon.

"Edgar! What the hell are you doing?" A deep voice rattled out of the darkness.

Bang! Zszs. Yet another ball of flame skyrocketed in an airborne game of tag with the first.

"Get that damn flare gun away from him! Edgar, you old drunk! I'm gonna kick your goddamn ass!"

Gabe sat up. Charlie grabbed his collar and slammed him to the floor.

Gabe smiled, proud as a new father. "I told you it would be all right."

Charlie untied Gabe's feet. "Oh, yeah? And just who's he signaling? Betty and her quilting bee?"

Beep, beep, beep, beep, beep, beep, sounded in the distance.

Aroogah. Aroogah, echoed from another direction.

"What the hell is that?" Charlie asked. "Chevy mating calls?"

"Fricks." A note of a chuckle tumbled out with the word.

Charlie ran his left hand over the barrel of the pistol and stared into Gabe's intensely satisfied eyes. "What's a Frick?"

"More trouble than any of these boys want to mess with." Gabe placed a hand on Charlie's forehead and brushed it over Charlie's wet hair. "Friends."

Aroogah. Aroogah. Beep, beep, beep. The clamor had united and was steadily drawing nearer.

"Tom!" a voice yelled. "Nobody said nothing about having to deal with the Fricks."

Out of the trees on the other side of the road came another's evident concern. "Yeah! I didn't plan on getting my head bashed in over a couple of queers, Tom! You better do something or I'm outta here."

"Everybody sit tight! I'll talk to Lester." The voice shook like Jell-O.

Amusement snorted out Charlie's nostrils. Whoever the Fricks were, they had some knees knocking out there in the dark.

A pair of engines roared, tires screeched. The motors eased their growls. *Thump thump.* The vehicles rumbled their way along the dirt road. A pinhole in a muffler spit a tinny chorus to the tension thick as river fog. Yellow light tented the truck bed. The motors stopped. Doors opened, then slammed closed.

"Gabe! You okay?" The snarl was throaty, deliberate.

"Lester, he's all right, but we need to talk."

"Shut the hell up, Tom. I don't have a damn thing to say to you right now. Gabe!"

The clap of assholes puckering overrode the crickets.

Gabe sat with his back against the truck's cab. "In the pickup. We're fine. I think Charlie shot Terry, though. Might want to check on him."

A rattled shout. "No, I'm okay. He missed. I fell off the truck."

Charlie pushed himself off the floor and sat next to Gabe. He holstered the pistol in his boot.

"Lester!" Gabe yelled. "Arnie and Phil have pistols."

Ka-chunk. Ka-chunk. Charlie's ears perked. *Shotguns. The Fricks don't play.*

"Arnie." Lester's words eased out calm, almost sedated. Charlie's muscles tightened. Just like Charlie, Lester obviously kept his wits about him when confronted with the extreme. "You boys better put those guns away unless you want to shoot yourselves every time you squat to take a shit."

"This is none of your business, Fricks." A new voice. Arnie?

"The hell it ain't, Arnie Andrews." Another new snarl. And this one sounded beyond merely pissed off. "You think you're getting out of here without me beating the tar out of you, you best do some rethinking."

"Oh, shit." Gabe sank down an inch or two and crossed his arms over his chest.

"What?" Charlie whispered. "What's going on?"

"That's Lester's daddy. Arnie cheated him on some spare parts twenty years ago. Sounds like he hasn't forgotten about it."

Bubbles of laughter leaked out of Charlie's throat.

Gabe turned to him; red measles of fear peppered his face. "You don't understand. Lester's daddy makes Lester look like a choir boy."

"They're queers, Carl! You come to help queers?" Arnie obviously wasn't done with the debate yet.

"Lester came to help his friend. I came to kick your ass, Arnie Andrews." Carl seethed the words. "My nephews came to help out if need be. A few of our cousins'll be along soon enough to clean up the mess."

"Cousins?" Charlie asked.

"Fricks ancestors used to sell whiskey to the Indians long before this county was formed. They're related to half the people around here. There could be one or a hundred on their way." His chin hit his chest. His eyes half closed. "I'm sorry."

"About what?" Charlie had no clue what Gabe had to be sorry about. Old Betty had come through, and then some.

"About the Indians." The man's eyes danced everywhere but to Charlie. "I meant no offense."

A rustle from the trees. Twigs snapped under feet. "Sorry, Tom." Charlie cocked his head. Yet another new voice. "Me, Jerry, and Rod got to side with family. We stand with cousin Carl. Oscar? What about you and your brothers?"

"Yup," Oscar replied. "Family comes first."

Six shadows stepped into the glow—six men ambled toward the headlights.

"You think I'm an Indian?" Charlie smirked. This was interesting.

Gabe's stare landed on Charlie's face. "Aren't you?" The gaze dropped to the floor. "I mean, it doesn't matter."

"Then it doesn't matter." Charlie stood.

"What do you mean it doesn't matter?" Gabe pushed his way to his feet. "Aren't you an Indian? I mean, I don't care if you are."

"Oh, sweet Jesus," Tom said. "This wasn't our idea, Carl. Perkins ordered this. We didn't want to do this. Gabe's one of us. He was born and raised here."

Charlie chuckled at the swing in denial of responsibility.

"So, are you?" Gabe asked.

Charlie leapt to the ground. "If you don't care, why ask?"

"Well, you know... some folks... some folks are prejudiced." The gulp echoed. "I'm not, of course. It's not important if you are an Indian."

"Then it's not important." Charlie took a step. "You going to introduce me?"

"Oh." Gabe scurried over the side to the ground. "How...." Another loud gulp. "Sorry. I didn't mean *how* like Indians say. What should I call you? Do you have an Indian name, like Eagle Feather or something?"

"Charlie Harris." He strode in the direction of the gaggle of men embraced by the headlights.

Gabe hurried alongside. "Are you an Indian, Charlie?"

"If it doesn't matter, it doesn't matter."

"You okay, Gabe?" the man big as a delivery truck asked.

"Damn it, Charlie. I need to know. Yeah. I'm okay, Lester. My head hurts, is all. They knocked us out—"

The pocked face scrunched to a mass of fury. "Who the hell hit Gabe? Get your ass over here!"

Footsteps clomped across the ground. A car door slammed, and an engine roared to life at the front of the line of parked vehicles. Tires spun on the dirt, and the car made a beeline down the road.

"Ronnie Smith," someone offered.

"I'll catch up with Ronnie later." The man cleared his throat and spat into the dirt.

Gabe made the introductions. "Lester, this is Charlie Harris. Charlie, Lester Fricks."

Charlie squinted an eye. Old Lester was huge. He glanced at the older man standing next to Lester. Old daddy wasn't. Lester towered an easy foot over his dad. But Carl was no slouch. The silver-haired man was solid as brick. Charlie grabbed Lester's extended massive paw. The leathery skin was smooth and hardened from labor. "Nice to meet you."

The two hills that served as shoulders shrugged. "Any friend of Gabe's is a friend of mine." He let go of Charlie's hand. "Good grip. Tough skin. You work hard for a living." The eyes scoured Charlie's face. "You've seen some stuff. Bad stuff. But you made it through. Glad we're on the same side." He nodded slowly. "Man would be a fool to tangle with you. How about I buy you a beer later? We can talk more."

Charlie smiled. Lester'd sized him up in the blink of an eye. Charlie liked him.

"They're queers, Lester," some brave, if not ignorant soul called out.

Lester's eyes turned to stone. "Gabe's my friend!" He glanced at Charlie. "And Charlie too! Anybody got a problem with that?"

"No, no, sir," a myriad of voices muttered.

Carl slapped Lester's arm. "I got some business to take care of." He turned toward the trees to his left. "Where the hell are you, Arnie?"

"In that clump of oak. I'll show you." One of the men behind Carl stepped forward and led the way.

"Tom," Lester said, "what's this all about?"

Captain Tom shuffled over. Maybe it was the light that gave him such a pale complexion, but Charlie figured the mammoth man confronting him probably had more to do with Tom's lack of color.

"Chief Perkins wanted us to bring Charlie out to the old Milford place."

Lester's eyes went dead cold. Charlie shivered. He'd seen the look before, in the faces of men about to kill with their hands.

"Why?" Lester hissed. "Perkins up there?"

Yeah. Why?

Tom shook his head. "I don't know who's supposed to be there. Perkins said we should rough up Charlie and take him there. Said we could do whatever we wanted with Gabe." His hands and fingers moved in the air as fast as his mouth. "We weren't going to hurt Gabe. I swear, Lester. We were just going to scare him a little. Christ, Lester, I swear."

"Perkins." The name blistered out of Lester's nose like snot.

"Eee!"

"Come back here, you asshole! I'm not finished with you yet."

Lester turned toward the trees. "Sounds like dad found Arnie."

"What's planned for me at this Milford place?" Charlie took a deep breath. He closed his eyes and rolled the odor of the firs, maples, and oaks over his tongue. Trees had flavor in their scents, and these tasted like home.

"I don't know. Honest," Tom answered. "That's all I know."

Charlie took another breath and held it in his lungs. A tack hammer of foreboding chipped at his brain. His stomach wrenched. Sweat dampened his palms. He rubbed his thumbs over the moisture. The hammer cracked the cluster of confusion he'd been carrying around in his mind. The reason behind the mysterious telegram fell through the fissure.

Charlie Harris had been summoned to Whistle Pass to die.

CHAPTER 21

"ROUGHED up, huh? How bad?" Charlie asked.

Gabe stared open-mouthed at Charlie. He couldn't be saying what he hoped he wasn't saying. Charlie couldn't be thinking about going through with this? Could he?

Captain Tom shifted his gaze to his feet. "Enough you can still stand, but can't fight so good."

Looking at Lester, Charlie slipped off his pea coat. "Let's get started."

"Oh hell no!" Gabe's stomach shriveled to a prune. His mind went numb as his knees. "You can't go up there. I won't let you!" How he could stop Charlie from doing anything, he had no idea, but he had to try.

"Excuse us a minute." Charlie gripped Gabe's elbow and pulled him along beside him to the back of the pickup truck.

Gabe's feet shuffled as if caked in concrete. He laid his arms over the tailgate for support. All feeling below his waist drained out his toes. He leaned further over the gate, notching it into his armpits so he wouldn't collapse. The fingers of Charlie's left hand massaged his neck; the right hand stroked his arm. Gabe fought back the need to fall into his arms.

"I have to go up there, Gabe. This won't be over if I don't. Whatever the real reason is why I'm here is at that old farm. Can you understand?"

Yeah. He understood, but that didn't change anything. "What if they kill you?"

Oh, Christ! What if they did kill him?

Charlie's hand swept down Gabe's arm to his hand and rubbed his fingers. His voice stayed eerily calm.

"This isn't just about the photograph. Even if Roger and Dora had it, I'd still be a threat to whatever their game is. They know I've got a weak spot now; a vulnerable spot they can hurt if I don't play ball. I have to end this tonight."

Gabe turned his head to look into Charlie's eyes. "What weak spot?"

The fingers on Gabe's neck pressed down. "You."

His heart twirled then tripped and fell flat on the ice. Charlie was going to quite possibly risk his life for Gabe. Nuh-uh. Not this night. Not ever.

At least, not alone. "I'm going with you."

Charlie's fingers on his neck squeezed into his skin. "No. You're staying here."

Gabe pushed away from the pickup and brushed Charlie's hand off him. "Mayor Black and some man from the power company brought you here to take care of some problem for them."

Charlie's hands jammed into his jeans pockets. His right eye narrowed.

"It's true, Charlie. Lester overheard them talking, but they didn't say what the problem is."

Charlie sighed. "Dora, I 'spect. This pistol in my boot belongs to her. She wants me to kill Roger."

Gabe's knees crumpled. He tossed an arm over the tailgate for support. "Jesus, Charlie. Why would she want you to commit murder?"

"Some land her father owns that Roger wants to build that nuclear plant on. She said she's afraid Roger will kill her father to get it built."

"No! Charlie, no." This wasn't right. Charlie couldn't have understood what she said. "Dora's dad died several years ago. He used to own the building the mayor's got his slot machines in. He was a farmer who retired to a tavern. When Roger came home from the war, he went to work as a bouncer for the old man."

Charlie chuckled. "I'll be damned." He pulled a hand out of his jeans and tugged at his beard. "They wouldn't know the truth if it crawled up their collective asses." His eyes narrowed. "You stay here."

"No." Gabe grinned. This was an argument he could win. "You wouldn't let me go in there by myself, and I'm not letting you go without me."

Charlie snorted. "You don't know what you're getting into."

"Neither do you." *Touché. Parry. Thrust.* "You said you think you love me. I know I love you. You go, I go. End of discussion."

"Lester!" Charlie shouted.

The big man clomped his way to them. "Yeah?"

Charlie didn't take his eyes off Gabe. "Gabe's coming with me. Just the head and faces. Just enough so we're groggy." He grinned again. "Don't damage those luscious lips. I have every intention of kissing them when this is over."

Gabe's heart melted.

"Ooh," Lester moaned. "I didn't need to know that."

Charlie transferred his gaze to Lester. "Don't be too far behind."

"I won't be. You got my word. But if Perkins is up there, he's mine. Deal?"

"Yeah. Fine."

Gabe smiled but tensed every muscle in his body. He was about to get the shit beat out of him by one of his best friends. Vomit boiled in his belly and rose like mercury. A wall of hand slammed into his face. The blow spun him, puke blew out his mouth. Lester jerked him around and slapped him again. He fell to his knees.

A hand lifted his chin. Gabe stared into Charlie's sorrowful eyes.

"I'm sorry, Gabe," Charlie whispered. His fist drew back. "You're not coming with me."

Charlie's punch to Gabe's jaw drew closed the curtains of consciousness.

CHARLIE'S eyelids fluttered, he rolled his head around on his neck. Old Lester packed a punch that left him feeling like wet cardboard on a highway.

"You okay, Charlie?" Lester asked.

"Yeah. Tie me up. Who's driving me up there?"

Lester wrapped rope around Charlie's forearms and knotted it. Charlie nodded approval at the magician's illusion. Sideshow magicians allowed local cops to add a final set of handcuffs to a series of them on the magician's wrists. That last set sat on the forearms. Once the magician removed his trick cuffs, he simply slid the last set, the ones he didn't have a key or slip button for, down his arms and off his hands—magic.

"One of my cousins. Edgar will be in the back of the truck with you. He'll have his flare gun if it all goes to hell in a handbag before we can get there. The signal flare might stall them just long enough."

"Yeah, well, don't be in too big a hurry. I'm pretty sure I'm supposed to get killed up there, but there's got to be a reason why this whole charade's taking place. Perkins could have put a bullet in my brain and dumped me in the river anytime Dora and Roger wanted him to."

"The more involved, the more to lose."

Charlie stared at the big man. "What do you mean?"

"You don't know these men that are here. They're the ones who keep complaining about the Fourth Street gambling. Most are family men, good men at heart. Hook 'em into a murder, and they won't have a choice but to keep their mouths shut and do what they're told. Easy enough to expand the gambling when the objectors clam up about it. Maybe some like Captain Tom would even have to bend over and put some machines in their businesses. With one man dead, nothing would prevent another from getting killed. Nobody'd want to be that next corpse."

Charlie curled a lip in admiration. Lester was big and had a brain to match. "How is it you're not the sheriff?"

"Pfft." Lester looked at the ground. "One man can't change much. I don't have the smarts for the job, anyways."

Charlie grabbed Lester's arm and turned him to face the throng of men idly watching. Tom and his band immediately straightened and stood tall.

"You're not alone. These men just need a leader they know won't turn their back on them. You're a fair man, Lester. You judge folks by their heart and their soul. Can't ask for more than that." Charlie climbed over the side of the pickup into the bed. "As for smarts, men don't willingly follow idiots. Especially me. And I'd follow you barefoot to hell and back." He turned toward Edgar. "Let's get this show on the road." He sat with his back against the cab.

Lester slapped the side of the truck. "You be careful up there. I got a feeling I'd never hear the end of it from Cathy if Gabe's fella got himself killed. And I'll think about the sheriff job."

The pickup lurched forward.

CHAPTER 22

LIMP tree branches and untrimmed nests of berry bushes scratched at the truck crawling along the dirt path. The pickup slowed, bumped over a half-buried log, then eased its way back to turtle speed. The darkness hung as heavy as the dank dampness dripping from the overgrowth. Forest musk of decaying wood, pine, berries, ferns, and wildflowers tugged at Charlie's senses, soothing the minor nerve that hadn't gotten the message he was headed into danger and he needed every bit of calm he could muster.

The beast inside him stirred, stretched, and waggled its claws in preparation of the fight for survival.

Charlie looked at the treetops tickling the sky… and smiled. If this was the one he didn't walk away from, he couldn't think of a better place to die. He kept his gaze on the few stars.

"Tell me about this place, Edgar."

"Same family owned it from the time the first cabin was built. Tough folks. Poachers, fish thieves, and the like. They'd rob commercial fishing lines on the river and sell the catch as their own. Around here, that could get a man killed. The Milfords didn't mind killing back if you got one of theirs. They turned to making shine during Prohibition. In the thirties, revenuers raided the place, and that was the end of the Milfords. The ones who didn't die in the gunfight or go to jail drifted away. Dora Black's daddy took the place over and used it as a hunting cabin. Roger still does. Only one truck path in, but there's hunting trails all over the place."

Charlie swung his gaze to Edgar. "Dora owns it?"

Edgar nodded. "Yes, sir."

Charlie returned to watching the stars. Roger and Dora could have a hell of a greeting planned for him.

"The Milford place is over the next rise," a voice called out from the cab.

"Punch me in the nose, Edgar."

"Huh? Why would I do that? Maybe you can't see them, but you got some marks on you from Lester."

Charlie turned his head toward the old man. "But no blood. Roger's not stupid."

Edgar sighed a stream of vapor that immediately disappeared in the chilly air. "Close your eyes. I can't do it with you watching me."

Charlie did as instructed. The blow stung fast and hard, like a cloud of hornets that found one spot to plant their stingers. His nose heated and ran. He swiped a hand across the base and opened his eyes to the blood-smeared fingers. Quickly, he wiped his hand clean on his right cheek and licked the copper-tasting blood around his lips.

He stared at Edgar. "Listen to me. They're going to try and kill me. Whoever's at this place isn't going to let you and that flare gun stick around to see it. When we stop, drop the gun over the side of the truck. I may need it."

Edgar's eyes narrowed in concern and apparent confusion. "What about the gun in your boot?"

"They'll find it." Charlie smiled. "In fact, I'm counting on it."

"House is coming up. Three man are walking out," the driver called.

"Put the hood on me, Edgar. Showtime." He wiped his brain clean. Any thoughts, any indication he had anything planned, might bring about his immediate death, and he needed to buy just a little bit of time. Gabe's face came to the forefront. Closing his eyes, he inhaled. A remembrance of Aqua Velva toyed with his bloody nostrils.

Edgar slid the hood over Charlie's head. "Good luck, soldier."

"Drag his ass out of there!" a surly voice snarled as the truck stopped.

"Perkins and two men I don't recognize," Edgar whispered. "No sign of the mayor."

Hands tugged at Charlie, pulled him over the side of the truck, and slammed him to ground hard as concrete.

"Get the hell out of here and forget you were ever here, or I swear I'll kill both of you and throw your dead asses in the river."

The engine roared. A tire spun. The pickup clanked and bumped its way out of hearing range.

A foot stomped Charlie's belly. He rolled to his side and went fetal. "Gack." A kick to the ribs. "Ooph!"

"Stop it! Get away from him." The new voice Charlie knew all too well. Roger.

"He's got something in his boot."

"Well, then take it out of his boot, Howard. Don't beat him to death," Roger ordered.

Howard. Police Chief Perkins. Charlie tightened his muscles, pulling his arms against the ropes to ensure the cop would believe his arms were secure and he was defenseless. His jeans leg was yanked upward, the pistol jerked from his boot.

"He's got a gun," Perkins growled.

"Give it to me." Seconds passed. Roger screamed his rage. "This is Dora's pistol. The bitch gave him her gun!"

The hood ripped over Charlie's face. Canvas scraped his skin. He looked into Roger's fierce eyes.

"You weren't thinking about killing me, were you, Charlie?" Roger stood. "Get him on his feet."

The two men he didn't know pulled him off the ground.

Roger patted Charlie's cheek. His eyes almost showed sincerity. Almost. "I'm sorry. I really am. You deserved better than this." He grabbed Charlie's arm and turned him, pulling him along beside him.

Charlie looked over his shoulder to see where the lane was, where the flare gun would be. Three leaning fence posts without fence marked the spot.

"Bring out the Kraut." Roger kept the pace steady until they stood in the center of a clearing. There they stopped.

Kraut? Charlie scanned the area. A ramshackle one-story house rested to his left. A barn, nearly collapsed on itself, sat thirty yards or so from his position. Trees bordered his right. To his left, shrouded in darkness, was the lane. What was missing were Perkins and the two men. He looked around, but they had vanished. Charlie glanced at Roger. *Shit.*

Roger was decked out in army fatigues.

Skree! Bang! Charlie spun toward the barn. *Skree!* A shower of sparks branched light into the clearing. *Bang!*

Bang, bang, bang, bang, bang. A bevy of sparks, red, yellow, white, skittered across the ground.

"Machine guns, Charlie!" Roger shouted. "Mortars!" *Skree! Bang!* "An ambush, Charlie. Jesus Christ! Where are they, Charlie? Which way should we run? Save us, Charlie!"

A wave of gray smoke ballooned out of the trees, deflated to the ground, and slithered across it. Explosions. Gunfire… screams. Bangs of guns echoed in his ears. The stench of gunpowder tore at his mind, shredded it.

"Argh." Roger doubled over, dropped to his knees. "I'm hit, Charlie. Help me. Save me, Charlie."

Charlie whirled. Scanned the area for where the attack would come from. "Stay low!"

"Run, men, run. Take cover," the LT yelled.

"No, LT. Stay low until we know where the attack's coming from." Charlie frantically searched for any sign of the enemy. Across the clearing, out of the barn came the first of the Germans. A slight built man, clad in German infantry gray and carrying a bayonet.

"There, Charlie. There. Here they come, Charlie. Help me," Roger pleaded.

Charlie crouched, focused his energy on the advancing soldier. He grabbed at his belt. His weapons had somehow become lost. Breath surged in and out of his chest. The beast within rose and shrieked its readiness for the attack. Charlie bolted forward, into the fray. If this was his day to die, as many Germans as he could kill would die with him.

He stretched out his legs to cross the ground as rapidly as he could. Guns fired. Machine guns chattered. Mortar rounds exploded. Smoke swirled around his feet. The lone German froze. Charlie dove headlong at the gray-clothed figure. He grabbed the hilt at the blade, yanked the hands holding the bayonet downward, then in toward the German. The bayonet fell free. Charlie kept his hold on the blade and drove it toward the German's belly.

Dora Black's tear and terror-filled eyes locked with Charlie's gaze as the bayonet slammed into the gray infantry coat cloaking her body.

"I'M NEVER going to forgive you, Lester," Gabe hissed.

"Not my idea, Gabe. But Charlie was right. He's been in the shit. You haven't." Lester slapped the cab of the truck. "Faster, Dad."

Gabe ducked in the truck bed. A low branch scraped over the steel of the cab's roof.

"Best stay down 'til we get there," Lester said.

The truck tires hit something and bounced into the air. Gabe hit the floor, then ricocheted up. Lester snatched him mid-flight and pulled him tight against the big man's bulk.

"Christ, Dad!"

"You want I should slow down?"

"No!" Gabe hollered. "Faster."

Bang, whiz, bang, bang.

Gabe sat upright. "Shit."

"Sounds like a war zone," Lester said.

A shiver quivered Gabe's shoulders. His throat parched. He thrust his hands together and dug fingernails into his skin. "Charlie suffers from shellshock. God only knows what he's going through up there."

Bang. Bang. Skree. Boom.

"Shellshock?"

"Yeah. It happened to him at the hotel." He avoided the part about climbing in bed with Charlie. "He really lost it. Thought he was back in the war."

"Faster, Daddy!"

"Hold on tight, boy!"

Lester grabbed the rim of the truck bed. Gabe grabbed Lester and hung on for dear life.

"GABE." Charlie muttered the name. "Gabe." The man's image came into dim view. "Gabe." The gentle features of the man with perfect hair sharpened. "Gabe."

Dora trembled in his grasp. Guttural words eked out of her. "Don't kill me. Please."

"Gabe." Gray eyes glistened. The soft, smooth lips parted, then smiled. Charlie leaned into the shaven face, rubbed his beard over the strong cheek. "Gabe."

"I'll be whoever you want me to be if you don't kill me. Please, Charlie. Let me go."

Charlie swallowed the stink of the fireworks popping around him and the smudge pots releasing smoke into the clearing. He looked down at the knife palmed broadside against the German infantry jacket. Smiling, he stared into Dora's petrified face. "Shut the hell up, Dora."

He dropped to the ground and relaxed his arms. The rope bindings loosened. Bringing up a foot, he kicked the rope down his coat sleeves and off his hands.

"Cut me loose." Dora extended her own bound hands.

"Kill her, Charlie, before she kills us!"

"You shut the hell up too, Roger." Charlie'd had enough of this shit. Time to get serious. He scrambled to his feet.

Roger steadily approached, his arm extended, Dora's pistol clutched in his hand. "You kill her or I will. Either way, you'll take the blame, Charlie."

Charlie shrugged. "Kill her. I don't give a damn about her."

"You asshole," Dora screamed.

"Have it your way." Roger squeezed the trigger. *Bang.* He fired again. *Bang.*

Dora shrieked and threw her arms over her body. "Oh, God. I'm shot! Help me. Somebody help me!"

Charlie rolled his eyes. "They're blanks, Dora. Cut the dramatics."

She patted her torso and opened an eye at him. "I'm not dead?"

"Not yet. But if you keep standing here, I can't promise you won't be." He sawed the bayonet through the ropes around her wrists.

"Kill the both of them," Roger snarled.

"You kill me and you get nothing," Dora hissed back at Roger.

Charlie turned and raised his brows at the woman. Maybe this wasn't going to work out so well after all.

Roger thrust a hand in the air. "Wait a minute. Nobody move." He glowered at Dora. "What do you mean I don't get anything?" His eyelids went heavy and drooped with his shoulders. "You changed your will."

"Damn right I did. I die of anything other than old age, and the only thing you get is the funeral bill."

Roger threw the pistol to the ground. The gun bounced and tumbled to a stop.

"Damn you! I can't trust you at all."

Charlie glanced to the barn. A shadow shifted. Whichever one of the men had pushed Dora out of the barn was still in there.

"Trust me? You were going to kill me, you butthead. I ought to cut you out of this deal all together."

Roger kicked the pistol across the ground. "You gave him your gun. Tell me you didn't want him to kill me. Tell me, bitch."

Charlie took a step toward the barn.

Dora's hands went to her waist. "Yeah. I wanted him to kill you. You were negotiating land prices without me. How dare you!"

"What'd you expect me to do? You were so busy jumping in bed with anybody you thought could get you a better price, you were literally screwing the whole thing out of existence. Even the power company wanted you out of the picture."

"Thurston? *Thurston?* No. I won't believe it."

Charlie took another step. The shadow moved again.

"Yeah. Even that old codger. Business is business, honey."

Dora turned her glare on Charlie. "Yes. Business is business. And your boyfriend here could still flush the whole thing down the toilet."

Charlie inched another step.

"What do you suggest?" Roger asked.

"A fifty-fifty split of the take. A legal, binding contract. After lover boy's out of the picture and no longer a threat."

Charlie cringed. All the parties had reached an agreement. Unfortunately, the deal hinged on him being dead. *Here we go.* He bolted for the barn.

"Get him!" Dora shouted.

The shadow morphed into the figure of a man. Charlie dove to the dirt floor, rolled, then raked a leg over the floor and swept the man off his feet. The man fell flat on his back. The impact reverberated through Charlie's body. Charlie sprang to his feet. He nailed a boot heel onto the wrist of the hand holding an automatic pistol. Jumping up, he drove a bent knee into the man's face. Hot blood dotted Charlie's cheeks. A muted groan, and the man's head slipped limp to the side.

Charlie reached for the pistol. A shot rang out. Bits of dirt erupted into the air. He abandoned the gun and ran toward a spot of dim light—a hole—in the back of the barn.

Another retort. Wood cracked above Charlie's head. A cloud of dust puffed down on him. He tumbled into the weeds and scurried through the barn's shadows. Angling left, he ran in the direction of the house.

Shouts flittered in the night. Cries directing men toward him echoed. He churned his legs past two parked cars, one being Roger's white T-bird, and a motorcycle. The three fence posts came into view.

"I see him!" *Bang.*

A bullet whizzed past.

Charlie lunged forward. He raked his fingers through the grass and weeds. Cold metal brushed his hand. His fingers snagged the flare gun. Dropping the bayonet, he twisted to a prone position, planted an elbow for stability, and took aim. The darkened figure of a man came in range. *Pop. Zsst.* A red fiery projectile branded the night.

"Aiee!" The man's chest lit up like sunrise on the river. Flames illuminated his face. The man tore at his burning coat, ripped it from his body, and slapped the smoking fragment to the ground. Screaming, the man fell and rolled back and forth over the weeds and dirt.

Charlie frowned his disappointment. This man wasn't Perkins, or Roger either.

A booted foot kicked Charlie's arm upward. The flare gun somersaulted away from him. He dipped and rolled. A second kick feathered his face. Charlie grabbed the foot and twisted. The attached body pivoted, then fell on top of him.

Fatigues. Roger.

Charlie sneered and let fly a fist into Roger's temple.

"Unhh," seeped out of Roger's mouth. The head turned slightly. Flames from the burning coat flickered in a glazed eye.

Charlie drove a full set of knuckles onto the back of Roger's neck. The body went abandoned-dishrag still.

Movement to his right, between Charlie and the fire. Something coming in fast. He raised his arm to ward off the blow. Leather and lead cracked across his shoulder. Pain exploded across his clavicle. *A sap. Perkins.* Instinctively, Charlie twisted left, but Roger's weight, splayed over him, pinned him. The sap came again. He threw his right arm backward and up. The blow glanced off his arm and across his skull.

Perkins sneered down at him. "Always wanted to beat a queer to death. Looks like you got elected, asshole."

Charlie reached out with his left hand for the bayonet. The handle nudged his fingertips. He clawed it into his hand. Perkins leveled another thrust of the sap. Charlie offered up his right shoulder, screamed in agony when the sap slammed into him, but the momentum aided to shift his torso right. Blindly, he swung the bayonet across his body.

A wash of yellow light bounced over Perkins, revealing his leg. Charlie turned his wrist and swung for the bleachers. The blade scraped bone, then dug into the thick, meaty calf. Perkins tilted right.

"Goddamn it." Perkins whirled and pulled the bayonet from his wounded leg. The light grew larger. Perkins looked up, his features jaundiced under the yellow glow. Blood glittered in streams on his pants leg.

A truck rattled and clattered up the lane. *Aroogah. Aroogah.* The light from the headlights bounced over the macabre scene.

Charlie zeroed in on the bloody wound and hammered a fist into it. Perkins leg quivered and sank, but the copper gathered enough strength to limp off.

A thud from behind the headlights. Lester bore down on the scene, a runaway locomotive of rage and muscle. "Perkins! I'm gonna kill you!"

A motorcycle cracked to life. The engine roared. A wheel spun. Charlie watched the headlight and tiny red taillight disappear through the trees.

"Son of a bitch," Lester heaved. He turned and dragged Roger off Charlie.

Gabe slid to the ground, grabbing Charlie in his arms. "You okay?"

Charlie's shoulder melted in painful heat. "I don't know." He rolled the injury. "Nothing broken, I don't think. But it's going to hurt like hell in the morning." He smiled at Gabe. "Thanks for coming. Not sure how much longer I could have held him off."

Lester stood tall, snorting frustration, his gaze fixed on the trees.

"This doesn't change anything." Dora's voice. And much too calm for Charlie's liking.

Charlie sat up and pivoted around on his butt to face her. "Really? How's that?" They'd just tried to kill him. He really wanted to know how Dora figured her plans hadn't been altered just a wee bit.

"You're trespassing. We have the right to defend ourselves against trespassers."

"What the hell are you talking about?" Gabe snarled. "You brought Charlie up here to kill him."

"Did I?" She crossed her arms across her gray army coat. "And what will the testimony be? That I tied you up and drove you up here? Or you instructed someone to tie you up and drive you up here? A subterfuge in your plot to discredit the greatest candidate for the office of state representative this area's had in the last twenty years. I'll wager you even told someone to beat you up so it looked like you were brought here against your will. And when the Whistle Pass chief of police attempted to arrest you, you stabbed him. I saw you do it, and I'll swear so from the witness stand."

Charlie chuckled. Gabe hissed. Lester kept his gaze glued to the trees.

Old Dora knew her stuff, and she had more than enough money to buy the best attorneys and jury she could find. Charlie shook his head. Roger moaned and rubbed his temples. Dora strode over and kicked her husband in the ribs.

"Get up," she growled. "Now, I want all of you off my property."

Roger rolled onto his side and mumbled, "Me too?"

Dora closed her eyes. "You are such an idiot." She wheeled and walked toward the house.

Charlie pulled Roger to his butt. The two men sat and looked at each other for seconds that stretched like months.

Roger finally dragged his hands over his face. "I guess this didn't turn out like I'd planned."

Charlie knew he should hate him, but he couldn't locate any emotion whatsoever for his former lover. "Guess not. I'm still alive. In your mind, that keeps me some kind of threat. So, now what?"

"Would you have ever told anybody about us, Charlie?" Roger's eyes drooped, his brow rose.

Charlie snorted. He understood. "This wasn't your idea, was it? My coming here was all Dora's doing."

Roger nodded twice. "She didn't trust you. Didn't want any loose ends lying about that could unseat me from the state office. I figured to take advantage of the situation and be rid of her whoring ass once and for all."

Charlie merely sucked in his lips and shook his head. This man, this whatever Roger had become, bordered on pathetic.

Lester turned toward them. "I want to find Perkins. I've got some personal business to settle with him."

Roger looked up. So did Charlie. Lester's eyes glowed with his bridled fury. The man was clearly hell-bent on something, and Howard Perkins sat at the center of the bull's-eye.

"Where would he go, Roger?" Charlie asked. "He probably figures he needs to get the hell out of town after this. I imagine he understands now you and Dora would sell him out as much as anybody to protect your plans for the nuclear plant."

"The Nugget." Roger's chest sank under a heavy sigh. "Perkins knows the combination to the office safe. There's probably ten, twelve thousand in cash."

Lester was on the move. Gabe helped Charlie to his feet, but Charlie tugged against Gabe's pull toward the truck.

Charlie dug a dime out of his pocket and stared at Roger. "Heads, you win. Tails, you lose." He flipped the coin into the air, then snatched it with his left hand and slapped it onto the back of his right. Lowering his hand, he revealed the coin to Roger. "Tails it is."

"What did I lose, Charlie?"

"Me." He turned and jogged with Gabe for the pickup.

Lester grabbed Gabe's and Charlie's hands and swung them into the bed. The truck turned around, then headed down the path.

CHAPTER 23

"WHAT did you mean Roger lost you?" The sour tone of jealousy rang in Gabe's ears, but now that he'd opened his mouth, he couldn't stop the diatribe. "You said you love me, but you still have feelings for Roger, don't you. I thought it was over between you two."

Charlie leaned his back against the opposite side of the truck with his arms stretched along the steel bed so his hands dangled. "It is, and has been."

"Do you two really have to discuss this kind of thing in front of me?" asked Lester. "I'm trying hard to be open-minded like Cathy told me to be, but this is getting a little more than I can handle. Makes me want to punch something."

Gabe gulped. Yeah, he did need to discuss this, but maybe testing Lester's patience under whatever was on his mind about Perkins wasn't such a wise decision. He opted for silence.

"Sorry, Lester," Charlie muttered. "How come you want Perkins so bad?"

Lester scowled beyond the tailgate. Ice coated his response. "Personal."

Gabe flicked his brows up, then down in an "I don't know" gesture to Charlie, because he didn't know what had gotten into Lester. His friend had never shown animosity toward Perkins in the past.

The truck arrived at the confluence of waiting bigots. Lester hopped out.

"Slide over, Dad. I'm driving." He slammed the door.

"What's going on?" Captain Tom asked.

The truck sped off.

Gabe shouted from the bed, "We're raiding the Nugget!"

Cars and pickups flicked to life. Hasty Y-turns produced a caravan of bobbing headlights trying to catch up.

Charlie slid over so his back was to the cab. Gabe joined him. The roar of the engine, pushing for every bit of speed it could muster, barely masked the rush of cold air sliding over the cab and across the bed.

"I need to know, Charlie. Do you love me?"

Charlie folded his hands in his lap. "Yeah, I'm pretty sure I do. I used to think I was in love with Roger, but you get me thinking about family and settling down. With Roger, I'd thought about a future, but it never really was clear what that future might be."

Gabe's heart swelled and thumped against his chest. His armpits dripped nervous sweat. Yeah, he loved Charlie and wanted him, but this Roger thing confused the heck out of him. "Then what did you mean Roger lost you?"

Charlie raised a hand and massaged his forehead. "I meant he lost my loyalty. Didn't matter to me that we were over. I wouldn't have done anything to hurt him. I owed him that much."

More than a touch of irritation thrummed muscles in Gabe's chest. "You decided to change your mind based on the toss of a coin? A dime?" Anger replaced the irritation. "Is that how you make decisions, by the flip of a dime? I thought the coin toss for the waitresses' tips was quaint, but the fact is, you can't think for yourself, can you?" Near rage slithered out of him. "What about me, Charlie? Would you wake up some morning and flip a coin about whether you wanted me anymore? Jesus Christ, Charlie! Is that all you have to give? A dime? What the hell? Is your heart engraved with Roosevelt's face?"

He crossed his arms and stuck his hands in his pits. It wasn't just to pout, his hands were cold. But the pout felt pretty damn good too. A man would be an ignorant fool to get involved with somebody who couldn't think for himself. A tear formed and dribbled down his cheek.

Charlie slid his hands into his coat pockets. His voice was steady, calm. "Yeah. That about covers it. When I don't know what to do, I flip a coin. Simple as that. And yeah, sooner or later I'll flip one about you too."

Gabe rolled left, showing Charlie his back. The hell with Charlie Harris. He was an Indian, anyway. Who would ever get involved with an Indian? He pinched his eyes closed. Tears coated his face. His heart plummeted into his hollow stomach. "I would," he whispered.

The streetlights of Whistle Pass zipped by. Lester hadn't slowed the truck so much as a foot per minute. *Screech*! The truck slid on the pavement. Gabe slammed into the side of the truck, Charlie fell against him as the truck careened left.

"What's he doing?" Gabe stuck his head up. "Oh shit! Get down!"

Gabe went flat and hugged Charlie to him. The truck veered left. Brakes ground to a stop. The pickup whined in reverse, stopped. The engine growled, gathered its strength. The brake released and the mass of steel rammed the doorway.

Concrete splintered. Broken blocks of cement rained into the truck bed. Dust billowed, filled Gabe's lungs. Tables crashed, chairs shattered. The truck slid to a stop. Gabe and Charlie leapt out of the bed. Lester was already several strides ahead of them, his daddy close behind.

Lester flung himself against the door at the end of the bar. It buckled, the hinges broke. Lester fell to the floor. Charlie stepped over the big man's back and charged through the next open doorway. Gabe bolted into the room on Charlie's heels.

Perkins, stunned, turned. In one hand was a canvas tote bag. The other hand was in the wall safe. The hand came out of the safe, but what the hand held wasn't money. Gabe grabbed Charlie's coat collar, gritted his teeth, and flung Charlie to the floor. The pistol fired. Searing pain tunneled through Gabe's chest. An aluminum foil taste of adrenaline coated his mouth. He sucked in air and clutched his breast. Lifting his hands, he saw blood.

Gabe looked down at Charlie. Another gunshot. A mountain of a man stepped in front of Gabe. Lester gasped but continued his frenzied attack. Gabe sank to his knees. Charlie grabbed him and pulled him onto his lap.

"Gabe!"

Gabe stared at his bloody hands, then to Charlie for an explanation of what was happening to him. The pain in his body numbed and faded. Charlie's face fuzzed and grayed. "Charlie," he mumbled. "Charlie?" He tried to focus, but Charlie shimmered and faded.

"I NEED an ambulance!" Charlie screamed.

"On it," Carl said.

Charlie laid Gabe flat and ripped open his jacket, then the T-shirt. The blood oozing from the wound didn't froth. The bullet had missed a lung. The hole rested up and to the right shoulder side of the heart. Charlie sighed a gush of relief. Nothing vital had been hit. As long as Gabe didn't give in to shock, he'd be okay.

He glanced up at Lester. "You all right? Where'd you get hit?"

"Shoulder. I'm fine." Lester looked at Perkins, who stood with the pistol barrel crammed in his mouth and Lester's finger rubbing the trigger. "Gabe dies, I'm going to turn you into a jigsaw puzzle."

Charlie hurried the words so the office didn't become Lester's private butcher shop. "Gabe will be fine. He fainted."

Lester's lips curled. "That would be just like him. He's got a bit of a glass jaw." The smirk disappeared. "Took a lot of guts to take that bullet for you."

"Yeah." Charlie stroked Gabe's hair, molding it back to the perfection the man required of the hairstyle. "He probably saved my life."

"Ambulance is on its way," Carl said.

"Thanks, Daddy," Lester muttered. He looked beyond Charlie. "You boys go ahead and break everything that can be broke. I think maybe I should run for sheriff. If you boys want a clean county, I'm going to need your help. Let's start right here."

"We're with you, Sheriff Fricks." The voice belonged to Captain Tom. "We'll get all the honest businessmen to support you. Come on, boys! Let's destroy this damn place."

"Tom," Charlie called out. A flurry of footsteps tromped down the stairs.

"Yeah, Charlie?"

"I know you didn't get your queers tonight. An hour from now, in the alley two blocks south of the hotel, there'll be one waiting for you. He's yours to do with whatever you want." He continued to stroke Gabe's hair. The man's breaths came slow but steady. Blood seeped in a thin line over Gabe's chest and down his ribs.

"You sure?" The voice quavered. "Maybe it's not such a good thing."

"Yeah," Charlie growled. "This one I'm sure about. He needs to be taught a lesson."

Crashes and bangs reverberated beneath them. Coins rattled and chinked across the basement floor.

"If you say so, Charlie. Me and a few of the boys will be there, if that's what you want."

"Yeah. It's what I want." He rubbed a hand over Gabe's brow. Leaning over, he pressed his lips on Gabe's forehead. The skin was cool and clammy. Charlie's stomach churned concern.

A siren wailed the ambulance's approach.

"Me and Perkins here got some business to attend to."

Charlie nodded. "Don't kill him, Lester. Folks might not like thinking their next sheriff is a murderer."

Lester barked a laugh. "That'll depend on Howard's water skills. Let's go, asshole."

Perkins backed out of the room, his arms wide and the pistol jammed in his mouth. Carl hustled after them. The siren abruptly stopped. The pickup roared to life; then the motor echoed out of the building. Metal, probably the front bumper, scraped across the floor. Two men in rubber boots, canvas firefighting trousers, and metal-buckled coats ran into the room. One carried a stretcher. Charlie stood and stepped away to let them work.

One glanced up at Charlie. "He should be okay. I saw a lot worse in Belgium when I was a corpsman with the 101st. We'll take him to the hospital. He'll probably need surgery to remove the bullet, but he should do fine. You going to meet us up there?"

"Got something to do first. Make sure somebody calls Betty from the hotel. Gabe will want her at the hospital." He turned and headed through the doorway.

In the bar, he walked around the counter, kicked aside a broken chair, and grabbed a pack of Lucky Strikes. He tore off a corner and tapped out a cigarette, then clenched the tip between his teeth. Black packs of matches advertising the Nugget in bold gold letters sat in a glass bowl. He grabbed a book and thumbed a match over the striker.

Charlie inhaled. The smoke tasted warm, fresh, and steadied the nerve or two unraveling from Gabe's being shot. He emptied his lungs in a long exhale. The smoke rolled, then merged with the cloud of dust drifting about the room. Taking another drag, he took note of the fact the police hadn't arrived on the scene, which was just fine with Charlie. Officer Phil Austin was outside somewhere waiting for him. Charlie blew out a cloud of whitish smoke and grinned.

Austin wasn't getting out of this unscathed. Not at all.

Charlie took another hit off the cigarette and stubbed it out on the bar next to another burn mark. He slipped out of his pea coat and laid it over the polished wood. His shoulder panged, so he rubbed the reddened skin and rolled the injured shoulder to loosen the tightness seeping into the bones. He bent his arms and worked them in and out under the ribbed, sleeveless T-shirt.

"Here goes nothing." Charlie walked out the massive hole in the wall that used to be a doorway.

An engine gunned down the street to his right. A white Chevy with a bubble-shaped red light on top. The city squad car. The beast inside him stirred.

"Not yet," Charlie said.

Headlights flashed on, and the car crept forward.

Charlie took a deep breath, then bolted left toward the main avenue. Tires squealed. The engine rumbled. Charlie lengthened his strides. He ran full speed across the avenue, the engine's noise closing the gap. He continued up Fourth Street. Headlights lit the ground at his feet. A wooden fence appeared between two houses to his left. He spun on a boot for it. He clenched the fence and vaulted over it. Running through the yard, a clothesline—"Shit!"—he ducked. The rope scraped his hair. He vaulted the back fence into another yard and exited onto Third Street.

Tires chirped, the engine slowed, then raced. A spotlight's glow reflected off houses. Charlie ran between two more houses. Making a left, he charged from between two brick homes and crossed Second Street. He glanced up the street.

The engine gunned a block north. The spotlight flickered between buildings.

Charlie stepped forward and tripped over a bush. "Crap." He pushed off the ground to his knees and brushed himself off.

The squad car lumbered around a corner. The headlights captured Charlie. The car zoomed toward him. Charlie leapt to his feet and ran toward the approaching car. The squad bounced over the curb onto the sidewalk. Charlie jumped and slid over the hood. He tumbled to the ground. Gathering his senses, he looked around, rolled to his feet, then broke into a run. The squad's backup lights flashed on. The stench of burned rubber filled the air. Charlie turned the corner and ran for Main Street.

He turned onto Main. The hotel was only a block away. He dug deeper for speed. Brakes ground, the engine slowed, then zoomed to life again.

Continuing north, he ran with all he had left. His legs burned, his shins ached.

Tires squealed behind him. Headlights bathed him. Charlie pulled his knees higher, kicked out his legs for every inch of sidewalk he could cover. At the end of the next street, he crossed the intersection and slowed slightly. The squad zoomed beside him, then bounded over the curb, skidding to a stop.

Charlie hit the car and used it to push off from and run the opposite direction. He rounded the corner, then ducked into the alley. The second floor porch came into view. He shinnied up a support post until he was able to grab the railing and swing onto the porch. Charlie dropped to his knees and sucked in air. His ragged lungs groaned against the onslaught of cold air. Rubbing his thighs, he waited for the squad car and Phil Austin.

The engine idled, then crept into the alley. The spotlight searched every shadow like a lighthouse beacon beckoning wayward ships. The car slowly rumbled into view.

Charlie pushed his way to his feet. He planted his hands on the railing.

Austin, once again, didn't check the porches with no visible stairway or access, just like the cop hadn't the night Charlie'd staked the porch out.

Charlie breathed through his nose. His body calmed. The beast stretched. The squad eased its way beneath the porch. Charlie gripped the railing, took in a final deep breath, then threw himself over the railing.

He slammed his heavy boots onto the roof of the car with his full weight. The metal bent and dented. The red lens of the rotating light dislodged and clattered to the ground.

"What the hell!"

Charlie jumped to the driver's side and grabbed a garbage can. He swung the steel receptacle against the door. Garbage showered the car and splattered the alley.

"Goddamn it!" Austin hollered.

Charlie tossed the can aside. Peering into the open window, the sight of Austin sitting there with rotting lettuce in his lap brought out a satisfied smirk. Charlie thrust a fist through the window. His knuckles smacked the cop's cheek. He drew back his right fist and let the left fly onto the man's mouth. Blood splattered. Austin's head slapped the back of the seat. His eyes fluttered. Blood flowed from shredded lips.

Charlie opened the door. Grabbing the cop's leather jacket, he yanked him out of the car. Austin blindly swung a fist. Charlie jerked back. Air brushed his face. Charlie hammered two quick thrusts into the man's side. Austin groaned and leaned left. Charlie beat a fist into the right side. Austin staggered, then fell back against the car.

Austin reached out, got a grip on Charlie's shoulders, and drove his forehead into Charlie's face. Charlie blinked. Pain pelted him like a hailstorm. Austin slammed his head into Charlie again. Charlie staggered backward.

"Nngh," slipped out of Austin's mouth.

Charlie readied for the telegraphed blow. It came from Austin's right hand. Charlie ducked. The fist and arm swept over him. Charlie shoved into the cop, hurling him against the car. The waist-length leather jacket rose, exposing the belt and trouser tops... and the cop's kidneys. Charlie turned his rage loose. Fist after fist drove into the man. He didn't stop the blows, even as Austin's knees buckled. The man sank to the pavement. Charlie straddled Austin, then rendered one last blow onto the base of his skull.

Air gushed out of the cop's limp body as Austin crumpled into unconsciousness.

Charlie swiped at his face. Blood smeared his hand. He pinched his nose closed and leaned his head back. Opening his mouth, he breathed heavily and deeply. The chilly air vibrated through him. The smog of Austin's head butts lifted, and Charlie's brain cleared.

"Phew," he heaved. Charlie lowered his hand and looked at Austin. "You said you didn't fight fair. Guess I should have told you, I don't either."

He grabbed Austin's ankles and dragged him into the shadows under the overhead porch. Charlie grimaced and rubbed his shoulder. Perkins and that sap had connected a bit more than he'd thought. Weariness crept inside him on a shiver of night air. Sleep would be necessary when he finished here. There should be a chair in Gabe's hospital room. He puffed his cheeks and blasted a breath.

"Okay, big boy. Time to get up close and personal."

Charlie unzipped the jacket and yanked it off. The shirt came next. Hairy, stretched-skin flab jiggled. "You oughta try a little exercise." He slipped off the shoes. The stench crinkled his nose. "Jeez. I didn't know decay started at the toes." Charlie tossed aside the gun belt. Then he unbuckled and jerked the trousers off the man. Boxers. They had to go.

For the first time, he wished he'd thought to bring gloves. The stench emanating from the underwear wasn't spoiled cologne.

"No wonder old Dora wouldn't bed your smelly ass."

He closed his eyes and slid off the boxers. Cracking open an eyelid, there was obviously another small—emphasis on "small"—reason why Dora hadn't shown the man any sexual interest.

Charlie went to the gun belt and unsnapped a brown leather case. Inside rested a gleaming pair of handcuffs. He pulled them out. At Austin's nude carcass, he clicked one cuff on the man's left wrist, reached around a wood support post, then clicked the other cuff on Austin's right wrist.

There was one more piece of ornamentation Officer Austin was long overdue in receiving. Charlie picked up the uniform trousers. The weighted sap lay in the hidden pocket. He left the mound of pale blubber on its stomach.

"This is going to hurt you a lot more than me." Charlie spread the man's ample, pimpled butt cheeks, looked at the leather and lead sap one last time, then shoved the handle up the cop's ass.

CHARLIE parked the squad car in front of city hall. He climbed out and locked the Chevy's doors. He slipped the keys into the mailbox.

A line of cars and trucks came down the street. Captain Tom held out his arms in an unspoken question from the back of a pickup. Charlie gave him a thumbs-up.

Tom shouted his glee. "Let's go get him, boys. Run the queer out on a rail!"

Hands waved from car windows, men pumped fists in the air in the beds of trucks. Charlie dutifully waved back. Something flew into the air out of a truck. Charlie's pea coat landed in the street. The cavalcade sped away. He snorted his bewilderment and retrieved his coat, grateful for the warmth, not to mention the fact one of them had thought to grab his coat off the bar. A few hours ago, he was the target of their bigoted minds. Now, anybody in the wrong place would fill their need for…. Having no idea what their *need* was, he could only shake his head. The way things stood right now, Charlie could probably attend the next Sunday T party and pull up a chair at the card table.

People confused the hell out of him. Trees never said much.

Charlie pulled the pea coat tight around him, then buttoned the buttons. He dug out a cigarette, lit the smoke. The hospital was a long way up—nearly straight up. But that's where Gabe was, and sitting beside Gabe was where Charlie was going to be.

CHAPTER 24

GABE sat upright. A chrome kidney-shaped pan lay at his side. He grabbed the pan and puked. The floodgates opened, and vomit flowed nonstop out his mouth and nose. The eruption subsided, and he collapsed onto a pillow. Betty leaned over him and wiped his face clean with a cool, wet cloth. His right arm was bound to his chest by bandages.

"There, there, now, my boy," she whispered. "It's just the ether. You're waking up and your body needs to get the gas out of your system. The doctors took the bullet out. You'll be fine."

She handed him a Kleenex, and he blew his nose empty of the sour taste. A fresh tissue quickly replaced the soiled one. That one he used to wipe his tongue. Betty quickly handed him a replacement. Gabe smiled, released a contented sigh, and relaxed under Betty's loving care. A mixed bag of bleach, chemicals, and faint wisps of food slowly replaced the stink of his puke.

"Welcome back. So, now you know."

Heat flushed Gabe's cheeks and scorched his ears. *Charlie.*

"Know what?" He looked around the room. Charlie sat on a metal chair in the corner by the open door. The nurses' station lay just beyond. Nurses in white dresses and aprons with starched paper caps pinned in their hair scurried about. So much activity, it had to be morning.

"What you'd do under fire."

Gabe frowned. "I nearly died." His toes wiggled his nervousness. The realization he really had almost died didn't give him any comfort.

"You saved Charlie's life," Betty cooed. "You're a hero."

Charlie shrugged and held out his open palms. "You're my hero, anyway." He grimaced and rubbed his right shoulder.

Concern wrenched Gabe's chest. "What's wrong with your shoulder?"

Charlie's lips tightened. "I don't know. Maybe Perkins gave a little better than I thought he did."

Perkins. Gabe pinched his eyes closed. The night's activities stepped through the haze in his brain. He opened his eyes. "What happened to Perkins after he shot me?"

Charlie shrugged again. "No idea. Lester took him out of the Nugget, and I haven't seen or heard of either of them since."

Cathy walked through the doorway. "Haven't heard anything about the police chief, but the whole town's gossiping about Officer Austin. Seems Captain Tom and his little band of bigots found the night cop dancing in an alley wearing nothing but the end of his sap sticking out his butt. Last anybody saw of him"—she moved her arms up and down—"he was covered in tar and feathers and pumping the bars on one of those little track-checking carts and hightailing it down the railroad tracks."

Gabe's belly jiggled with laughter. "Ooh," he groaned as pain stabbed his chest.

Cathy leaned over and kissed Gabe on the cheek. She eased down on the edge of the bed. "There's more. There're some reporters and photographers from the *Chicago Tribune* asking a lot of questions about Mayor and Missus Black and the nuclear power plant. They've got city hall staked out. Mayor locked the doors and has a policeman standing guard. There's another reporter sitting in the hotel lobby like he's waiting for something to happen."

Charlie stood. "Gabe, I need the picture back."

Gabe glared at Charlie. "That's all you came here for, isn't it? You just wanted the picture. You didn't come here because you were worried about me, did you?" Anger and hurt spilled out. "What'd you do, Charlie? Flip your little coin and call the reporters? And now you want your little picture so you can leave town and go back to the reservation and chop down trees with your little tomahawk. Did you flip a coin about me yet, Charlie? Huh? Did you?"

"No, but we can fix that right now." Sarcasm oozed out of the man. He pushed back his open coat and dug in his jeans pocket. When he pulled out his hand, he held a dime. With his thumb, he flipped the coin into the air. Light glinted off the tumbling metal. Charlie snatched the dime mid-flight, then slapped it onto the back of his hand. He showed the results to Gabe. "Tails. I want the picture, Gabe."

"Screw you, Charlie."

Charlie turned toward the door.

"Wait a minute." Gabe loosed a long breath. The photograph didn't belong to him. It was Charlie's property. "Above my bed in the crown molding. There's an extra door key under the hotel check-in counter."

Charlie nodded and entered the hallway.

A hand cracked his cheek. "Ow." Betty glowered at him. "What was that for?" She slapped him again. A tear pearled in his eye. "Ow! Stop it. Why'd you do that?"

"Because you don't know why I slapped you the first time." She looked at Cathy. "I better get to the hotel. *Somebody* has to be in charge."

Cathy nodded. "I'll babysit our boy."

Betty stomped out of the room.

Gabe flared a nostril. "I don't need a babysitter."

Cathy patted the sheet over his legs. "Yes, you do. That little tantrum confirmed it." She pivoted to face him. "Look, Gabe. I don't know what this picture is you two were talking about, but I assume it's important or you wouldn't be hiding it in your room." She reached over and palmed his cheek.

Warmth flooded Gabe's face. Cathy was the big sister he'd never had.

"Put your emotions in check and think about this for a minute. There's a reporter from Chicago camped out in the hotel lobby. Charlie wants the photograph. Add two and two, Gabe."

A shiver rattled from the back of Gabe's neck all the way to the soles of his feet and back again. "He's going to give it to the reporter."

Cathy nodded agreement. "Uh-huh. Do you really think the reporter would be sitting there if he didn't already know the picture was coming?"

Gabe pushed his head into the pillow. The cotton pillowcase brushed his ears, the pointed end of a feather ticked his skin. "Oh, no." He sat upright and blinked at the dizziness. "We have to stop him. Cathy"—he pleaded for her help with his eyes—"that picture could destroy Charlie as well as the mayor."

Her brow drooped. "What's so important about this picture?"

He kicked off the covers. Cathy quickly pulled the hospital gown to his knees.

"Charlie and the mayor had an affair during the war. The picture is the two of them kissing."

Her mouth hung open, her eyes glazed. Fingers twisted his gown.

"I'm serious, Cathy. Charlie flipped a coin last night and told the mayor he'd lost Charlie. Later he told me that what the mayor lost was Charlie's loyalty. Charlie's sacrificing himself to take down Roger Black. Help me, please."

Cathy stood and pressed a hand on the bed to steady herself. She massaged her eyes before answering. "I'll talk to the nurses. Then we'll get you dressed and out of here."

Gabe swung his legs over the side of the bed and waited for Cathy's return. Each passing minute had become a precious commodity he couldn't afford to lose. Charlie Harris and his life decisions by coin toss wasn't someone he could build a future with, but that didn't mean he didn't still love the man and wanted him safe. And a newspaper-headline homosexual, probably an Indian on top of it, could never be safe. Unless….

Gabe rubbed his brow. He'd heard there was a community of homosexuals in San Francisco somewhere. Supposedly, they even had their own magazine, and nobody had burned the place down yet. If he could convince Charlie to go there, maybe he'd be safe. He clamped his hand over his forehead and squeezed. "Is there anybody who could convince Charlie Harris to do anything?" he mumbled to the white walls.

Cathy hustled into the room. "The nurse is calling the doctor to authorize your discharge. I'll help you dress."

A pang shot through his chest. He clenched his teeth and scrunched his face. Tears flowed down his cheeks.

Cathy put an arm around him. He buried his face in her shoulder.

"Gabe, what's wrong?"

He sought the comfort of her soul. His words fell out in a heavy, painful breath. "We're too late."

CATHY sped along the street and let the car plunge like a boulder down hospital hill into the blanket of fog covering the town below. Gabe's eyelids sank back in his skull. Tires screeched at every sudden curve in the nearly perpendicular route.

"Don't kill us, Cathy." Terror vibrated his throat, trilled his words.

"Oh, shut up, Gabriel," she growled.

He snapped her a look. Cathy had never, ever told him to "shut up" before. "What's going on with you?"

Her hands strangled the steering wheel of the old Ford. "Lester didn't come by to take Richie to school. I tried to call him again from the hospital, but there's still no answer at his house. When I called his folks' house, his mom said she hadn't heard from him or Carl. I'm worried."

Gabe rubbed his boots over the metal floorboard. Yeah. Something was definitely wrong, but Lester'd been on a crusade about Perkins last night. Hard to say what could have happened. No better time to find out the possibilities. "What's Lester so mad at Perkins about?"

She tugged at the blue lace scarf around her neck. Her left hand jerked the steering wheel into an S curve that exploded out of the mist. Gabe fell over the seat. She jerked the wheel the opposite direction, and he flopped against the door.

"Jesus, Cathy. You're not a stunt pilot."

The car plummeted the remainder of the steep hill. Her foot slammed down the brake pedal. Brakes ground, metal on metal. The stink of burning rubber filled the car's interior. The car lurched to a halt at the stop sign for Main Street.

She hesitated at the intersection. A shaky hand wiped her eyes.

"I never told anyone who Richie's father was...." Her voice dripped into sobs. Her body shook. "He said he'd kill my baby if I ever did."

"Oh, no." A flashbulb of comprehension popped in Gabe's brain. "Perkins. But not by choice. He raped you. And now, for whatever reason, you told Lester."

Her head barely moved from side to side. "I didn't want any secrets between us. Lester needed to know. Now I'm scared he might have killed Perkins."

He had no idea how to answer. Yeah, given this news, the possibility was very real.

Swiping at her tears, she eased her foot off the clutch and turned the car onto Main. Cathy clicked on the wipers against the wet gray cloud engulfing them. The blades thumped a beat as unsteady as Gabe's worried heart. Beads of water slithered up the sides of the windshield. Two of his few friends were in trouble—he chewed his lip—and he didn't know how to help.

The corner of the hotel and metal L hanging from an iron bracket broke through the dense fog. Cathy pulled the Ford into a parking space and turned off the engine.

Gabe sucked in two quick breaths, followed by a long, slow, even one to calm fraying nerves. He opened the door.

CHAPTER 25

BETTY stood waiting at the hotel's entrance. The forlorn look etched on her face told it all before she said a word.

"They're gone. I tried to stop Charlie, but he walked out of here with the reporter. I don't know where they went. They disappeared in the fog. I'm sorry, Gabriel." She gently placed her arms around him and pulled him to her. Her fingers stroked his disheveled hair. "I am so sorry."

He was too late. But he'd sensed that at the hospital. Gabe's heart twisted, and a tear rolled down his face onto Betty's dress. She patted his back.

"Come with me. You need to eat something. I made sure a table was ready for us next door."

"I'm not hungry." He stood straight. Cathy grabbed his arm and pulled while Betty gently pushed him from the other side.

"It's not open for discussion, young man," Betty said.

Cathy looked around him at Betty. "Has anybody heard anything about Lester or his dad?"

Betty clicked the thumb latch on the door handle and opened the door. "He was here."

Gabe stopped in mid-step and stared at Betty. "Lester?"

"Lester?" Cathy echoed. Her voice rose an octave. "At the hotel?"

"Yes. He left with Charlie and the reporter." She snickered. "If you don't mind my saying so, the man looked a fright. Soaked to the bone he was, like he'd been swimming."

Cathy threw herself into Gabe's arms. His chest and shoulder shrieked pain. Cathy immediately pushed away.

"I'm sorry, Gabe. Did I hurt you?"

He shook his head. "Nah. I'm just glad Lester's all right."

Cathy bounced on her toes. A smile parted her lips. "My teddy bear's alive."

Gabe glared at her from under lowered brows. "Teddy bear?"

She slapped his arm and wagged a finger at him. "Don't you dare tell him I told you I call him that."

He didn't fight the grin. "What do I get if I don't?"

"You don't get beat. Let's go eat. I'm suddenly hungry." Cathy led the way out the door.

The restaurant was filled with the usual railroaders and a few locals. Smoke drifted in a cloud at the tin ceiling. A collage of voices melded to a din of sound mixed with silverware ticking on plates. A table for four near the entrance sat awaiting guests. A "Reserved" sign hastily scrawled in black marker on an index card leaned against the sugar shaker. The trio pulled out chairs and sat.

The waitress, Freda, scurried to the table, her face a carnival of emotion. "Did you hear the news?" she gushed out in a torrent of tobacco breath. She repeatedly tapped the tip of a pencil on her order pad. "I just got off the phone with Becky. Everyone's talking about it."

Gabe sighed and shook his head. He didn't know how much more news he could handle.

"What news?" Betty asked.

"Some commercial fishermen found Chief Perkins washed up on a river bank about twenty miles south of here."

"Oh, God, no," Cathy cried. "No!" The room fell silent as stone.

Betty leaned over and hugged Cathy. "Shh. It will be all right."

Cathy broke out in body-shaking sobs.

Freda scowled. "It's not like he's dead or anything, Cathy. Jeez. When did you care so much about Chief Perkins?"

"He's not dead?" Gabe quirked an eye at Freda. "But you said he was washed up on a bank."

Freda stuck the pad and pencil in her apron. "Yeah, he was. They found him with his feet tied to the back of a rowboat caught in a snag of driftwood." She giggled. "They say he was plum naked as a jaybird, his hands handcuffed together over his head with a rope strung from the cuffs down his back to his feet, and begging for somebody to turn him loose."

Gabe cringed. "So, he'll be coming back to Whistle Pass." This wasn't good. Perkins would declare war on the whole county for this. Lester and his dad had screwed up big time.

Freda stroked her chin. "Mmm. Doubt that. They say somebody carved *RAPIST* on his forehead." A chuckle caught in her throat. "Bet that leaves a mark. If it's true, and Becky would be the one to know, her working at the phone company and all—you know she listens in on everything everybody says. That woman gossips more than—"

"Freda!" Betty barked. "Stick to the story."

Freda glared at Betty. "I'm just saying, if it's true, the man would be a fool to come back here, what with the vigilantes." She leaned over the table. A wash of toilet water rolled off her skin. Gabe's nose burned against the olfactory onslaught. The waitress's voice dropped to a whisper. "You heard the vigilantes ran that jerk Officer Austin out of town? They say he was caught doing the Sugar Plum Fairy dance on Main Street, naked as the day he was hatched. Who would have guessed? It just goes to show, you never know these days." She glanced at Gabe. "No offense, hon. You're not like them queers we hear about. You're one of us."

Gabe rolled his eyes. The whole danged town *did* know he was a homosexual.

"So, Perkins is alive?" Cathy shivered.

Freda slapped her hands to her waist. "Yes, sweetie. What is it with you? I've never heard you utter one kind word about the police chief in all the years I've known you."

"Yes!" Cathy played the table like bongos. Her feet stomped accompaniment. "Hee hee! He's alive!" She stopped abruptly and glared at the room. "Eat your breakfasts and mind your own damn business."

Forks and knives clattered on plates. Grumbles evolved into muttered conversations. The din quickly returned to normal volume.

Gabe looked at Freda. "It's a long story."

Freda scoffed. "Well, I don't have time to listen right now. What'll you have?" She pulled out the pad and pencil. The pencil lead left yet another smudge on the stained cotton.

In his heart, Gabe was thrilled for Cathy and Lester, but none of the news about Perkins changed Charlie's situation. He massaged a subtle throb in his temples.

Oh, Charlie. I wish there was something I could do.

A hiss of hydraulics leaked through the seams in the doorway. Gabe looked out the window. The ribbed metal side of a bus scattered the sodden fog. The black wheels rolled to a stop. The back of the bus sat visible out the window. The diesel engine hummed. Dense black exhaust mingled with the fog's gray.

"Coffee for me, is all," Gabe said.

"Bring him a sliced orange too ," added Cathy.

"And buttered toast." With a pat to his hand, Betty snagged his attention. "Farm butter's good for the digestive tract."

Gabe sniggered. "I have two mothers now?"

"If necessary." Cathy turned to Freda. "I'll have the farmer's plate. Extra sausage. And a large orange juice."

"Aren't we the little pig this morning?" Freda scribbled the order. "Betty?"

"Grape juice, a bran muffin, and extra butter. I'm trying to watch my weight."

"Right," Freda said and walked away.

Dejected, Gabe slumped in his chair. Betty rubbed his arm. "It will work out, Gabriel. Whatever path Charlie is supposed to travel, that's what will happen. God has a plan for every one of us."

"Yeah, right." He reached out and adjusted the salt and pepper to equidistance from the sugar shaker. Then he adjusted the containers to align with the chrome napkin holder.

"Maybe if you came to church with me some Sunday, you would learn these things, Gabriel."

Gabe snorted. "Please, Betty, I'm not really up to this right now."

The hum of the motor outside built to a crescendo. Black residue overpowered the fog. A hiss of air, and the bus pulled away. Gray mist quickly reclaimed the empty curb line.

"Think about it. That's all I ask, Gabriel."

He pouted his lips. "Yeah, okay. I'll think about it."

The door opened. Cathy shrieked and jumped so hard, the chair tumbled over. Then she launched herself at Lester. She hung like a human necklace around Lester's thick neck, her knees bent and swinging back and forth. Lester planted a kiss on her that made Gabe flush with heat and look away. A scrape of chair legs, and Gabe returned his gaze to Lester. Lester sat at the table. Cathy, though in a separate chair, refused to let loose of the man's arm. She glued her head to his shoulder.

Gabe tried to speak, but nothing came out.

"Charlie?" Betty asked for him.

Lester shook his head. "Gone. He just left on that bus."

Cathy covered her mouth with her hand. "Oh, no. I'm sorry, Gabe."

Gabe closed his eyes and lowered his chin to his chest. Any hope, any prayer, had just rolled out of his life. Resentment, anger, and heartbreak pushed rancid words past the dryness in his throat. "What did he do, flip a coin, and I lost?"

"No." Metal chinked on the table. "He told me to tell you to flip your own future."

Gabe slowly opened his eyes. Two dimes lay on the table; one heads up, the other tails up. He snorted. "A real comedian, isn't he?" The question came out a low growl. *The hell with you, Charlie Harris.*

Cathy picked up the dime displaying heads and turned it over in her palm. She quickly grabbed the tails up dime and turned it over in her palm as well. She looked at Gabe. "You said Charlie makes all his decisions on the toss of a coin?"

"Yeah. You saw it in here when he tossed a dime to decide if you got a tip. Hell of way to live, huh? Leaving all your decisions to chance. Not my idea of planning for the future."

"Did you ever notice we always won a tip from him, Gabe? Every single time." She spun a dime on the table. The coin whirled. "Heads."

Gabe tilted his head at her. She nodded toward the coin. It slowed, tracked a circular line, and fell over. Heads.

Cathy tossed the other coin onto the table. It bounced and rolled. "Tails." The coin, as if willingly obeying her every command, flopped tails up. She pointed her chin at the coins. "You might want to take a gander at those dimes."

Gabe picked up the coin displaying heads. Between his forefinger and thumb, he turned it over. Heads. He turned it over again. Heads.

He snatched up the tails dime. Tails on both sides.

Betty folded her hands on the table and gave Gabe a satisfied, smug expression. "It would appear Mr. Harris never left anything to chance after all, Gabriel. Until now. Which coin would you like, Gabriel? The choice has been left for you to make."

Burning emptiness scorched his soul and heart. Gabe bolted out the door. He stood on the sidewalk, straining his vision into the thick fog. Even if the bus had still been close enough to see on a clear day, the fog had erased every trace but a lingering scent of diesel fuel. Gabe slapped his hand against his leg. *Damnit!*

A shrill whistle scratched out of the dank cloud surrounding him. A second soon followed.

"Two freighters are doing a whistle pass," Betty said behind him. "Is that how you intend to leave this, Gabriel? You and Mr. Harris were but two lonely hearts conducting a whistle pass through the fog of your lives?"

He ground a palm heel into his eye to mash the welling tears. "I don't have any idea where he's going."

"Me either," Lester said. "But that bus he's on is headed for Charlton City. Least that's what was on the display board."

Cathy walked around Gabe. Pulling him into an embrace, she whispered in his ear, "Charlie's in for a rough time wherever he goes,

Gabe. Anyone with him, well, it won't be any easier for them, either. But they'd have each other to lean on. My car's around the corner."

Her fingers pried his fist open. Two small metal objects dropped into his hand.

"Choose your coin, Gabe."

CHAPTER 26

CHARLIE scratched his beard and leaned back in the seat to stare out at the grayness swirling past the window. Ripe as he smelled, the seat next to him would probably stay empty the entire trip to Charlton City. Where he went from there... he hadn't figured that part out yet. Random drops of moisture beaded and trailed up and back on the glass. He dug the pack of Luckies out of his pea coat pocket, then tapped out the tip of a cigarette. The end between his teeth, he pulled out the cigarette and lit it from a matchbook. He stared at the closed cover: "The Nugget."

Had it only been a few hours ago? The events already felt as distant as the war in Europe. He stuffed the smokes and matches back in his pocket and looked at the ceiling.

Smoke eased out of his mouth, rose in a spiral, then floated along the metal ceiling. Paper rattled across the aisle. An old man had turned the page of a newspaper.

Charlie chuckled softly and wondered how the codger would react to tomorrow's headline and photo. Roger Black's political career was as dead and flat as roadkill. The reporter had shared with Charlie, when they went to speak with Dora, she'd only stated her attorneys were filing for divorce, and any other comment would be through those same attorneys. By the time the *Chicago Trib* got through with the Blacks, Roger'd be broke and in hiding, and there wouldn't be a business in the country that would want to be tied to old Dora. She'd own a patch of farmland and not much else. If she still owned the land after the Feds got done with her in the ensuing gambling investigation.

The nuclear plant would still be built... somewhere. Just not anywhere near Whistle Pass.

He took another drag, then blew it at the recessed ceiling lamp.

And all this success had cost him was pretty much everything. There wouldn't be a backyard bigot in the country who didn't have a burning cross with his name emblazoned on it. Eventually, the fuss would die down; the public would find new names to vilify. Maybe then he could go back to the logging camp.

But he still wouldn't have Gabe.

Gabe was better off in Whistle Pass. Safer. Home was always safer.

Brakes ground and hissed. The bus slowed, only to pull off the highway. Charlie settled in his seat and took another hit off the smoke. Whatever this problem might be belonged to the driver, Charlie'd had more than his share for a lifetime. He rubbed his aching shoulder.

"What the hell do you think you're doing stopping my bus?"

Charlie chuckled. Somebody had managed to unleash the driver's ire.

"You see this? It's a badge. You're still in my county, so cool your props, Sky King."

That surly growl he knew. Charlie sat up. The front of the bus had been filled with Lester Fricks. Gabe pushed past Lester and stormed down the aisle, an empty coat sleeve bouncing with each step. Charlie's breath caught in his chest, right where his heart had stopped.

Gabe flipped a coin off his thumb. The tumbling metal arced over two seats toward Charlie. Charlie reached up and caught the dime. He looked at it and smiled. Heads.

Gabe flopped into the seat next to him. "Want to tell me where you're headed?"

Charlie shrugged. "I don't know. Can't live in big cities. I'd lose my mind. Too trapped. Thought maybe I could find work on a farm or ranch or something. Anything outdoors."

"Sounds good to me." Gabe sat back and waved his one free hand. Lester waved back and lumbered off the bus. Keeping his gaze straight ahead, he said, "Lester wanted me to tell you, once he's sheriff, you've got a job anytime you want one." His eyes turned toward Charlie. "You being a veteran and all."

Charlie sighed. This might be his dream come true, but Gabe didn't fully understand what he was getting into.

"It's going to get rough before it gets easier, Gabe. Maybe you should wait in Whistle Pass." A smile curled his lips, a smile that Gabe really was willing to walk away from his life—for Charlie. "Besides, you don't know anything about working outdoors."

"Nope, I don't." Gabe crossed his arm over the one strapped to his chest. "But I know how to keep books, and every business needs bookkeepers. The rest we can deal with together."

Charlie rubbed the back of his head over the seat. "It could get rougher than Whistle Pass."

Gabe shifted his body to face Charlie. His gray eyes glistened. "Then we shouldn't run out of things to talk about. At night. In bed."

Charlie's heart smiled as big as his mouth. "You're really serious about this?"

Gabe nodded. "More than anything, Charlie, I want to spend my life with you."

A loud hiss rattled metal below them. The engine revved, and the bus pulled onto the highway.

"Me too, Gabe. I love you."

"There's one little thing I need to know."

Charlie cocked his head. "What?"

Deep lines furrowed Gabe's face. "Are you an Indian?"

KEVAD is David "DA" Kentner, prolific author of romance, suspense, horror, and fantasy, and winner of American Mensa Ltd.'s *Calliope* magazine 18th annual fiction competition. His weekly column "The Readers' Writers" in which he interviews famous and soon-to-be-famous authors appears in newspapers across the country.

When not writing, shoveling snow, or mowing their five acres outside Freeport, Illinois, he's trying to explain to his wife that the TV has more than SOAP and GAME channels, and pizza really is a necessary and required food group.

You can contact KevaD at dakentner@yahoo.com or follow him on his web site http://www.kevad.net/ or Facebook: http://www.facebook.com/home.php#!/profile.php?id=100000734965695.